THE *Best* {BRITISH} *Short Stories* 2013

NICHOLAS ROYLE IS the author of more than 100 short stories, two novellas and seven novels, most recently *First Novel* (Jonathan Cape). His short story collection, *Mortality* (Serpent's Tail), was shortlisted for the inaugural Edge Hill Prize. He has edited sixteen anthologies of short stories, including *A Book of Two Halves* (Gollancz), *The Time Out Book of New York Short Stories* (Penguin), *'68: New Stories by Children of the Revolution* (Salt) and *Murmurations: An Anthology of Uncanny Stories About Birds* (Two Ravens Press). A senior lecturer in creative writing at the Manchester Writing School at MMU and a judge of the Manchester Fiction Prize, he reviews fiction for the *Independent* and the *Warwick Review*. A new collection of short stories, *London Labyrinth* (No Exit Press), is forthcoming. He also runs Nightjar Press, publishing original short stories as signed, limited-edition chapbooks.

Also by Nicholas Royle:

NOVELS

Counterparts
Saxophone Dreams
The Matter of the Heart
The Director's Cut
Antwerp
Regicide
First Novel

NOVELLAS

The Appetite
The Enigma of Departure

SHORT STORIES

Mortality

ANTHOLOGIES (as editor)

Darklands
Darklands 2
A Book of Two Halves
The Tiger Garden: A Book of Writers' Dreams
The Time Out Book of New York Short Stories
The Ex Files: New Stories About Old Flames
The Agony & the Ecstasy: New Writing for the World Cup
Neonlit: Time Out Book of New Writing
The Time Out Book of Paris Short Stories
Neonlit: Time Out Book of New Writing Volume 2
The Time Out Book of London Short Stories Volume 2
Dreams Never End
'68: New Stories From Children of the Revolution
The Best British Short Stories 2011
Murmurations: An Anthology of Uncanny Stories About Birds
The Best British Short Stories 2012

THE *Best* {BRITISH} *Short Stories* 2013

SERIES EDITOR **NICHOLAS ROYLE**

CROMER

PUBLISHED BY SALT PUBLISHING
12 Norwich Road, Cromer, Norfolk NR27 0AX

First published by Salt Publishing, 2013

Printed in Great Britain by Clays Ltd, St Ives plc

Typeset in Paperback 9/12

ISBN 978 1 907773 47 1 paperback

1 3 5 7 9 8 6 4 2

In memory of John Royle (1938–2013)

INTRODUCTION

FLASH FICTION. WAS ever an uglier, more inappropriate term coined to describe a literary form? For years, it seemed, we read about and heard about short short stories, short-short stories (subtly different, presumably), very short stories, micro-fictions, flash fiction and so on. At some point 'flash fiction' began to take hold and it does now seem to be the most widely used term, with its own Wikipedia entry, numerous prizes (including Salt's) and even a National Flash-Fiction Day.

I can count on the fingers of one hand the number of writers whom I have read who have published pieces of genuine merit that come in under, say, 1000 words. Lydia Davis is celebrated, with good reason; Kafka left a lot of very short, highly effective pieces. David Gaffney is, I think, one of very few contemporary British writers who have mastered the very short form. I loved his story 'Junctions One to Four Were Never Built', which was published in 2011, but couldn't quite see how something so short could occupy a place in last year's anthology alongside stories that were so much longer. Well, more fool me. Alison Moore's irresistible 'The Smell of the Slaughterhouse', which opens the current volume, is not very much longer.

Flash fiction is still an awful term. It hardly implies lasting value. But then, given that a lot of so-called flash fiction is not particularly good, maybe it isn't so inappropriate after all. Whatever term might be used to describe them, there are a few more really-rather-short stories in the current volume than in the previous two years. A careful reader might also suspect a bias this year towards experimental fiction. There was, in fact, no bias towards anything in my selection process, unless towards good writing, and good writing often involves taking risks.

The stories reprinted herein first appeared in literary magazines such as *Ambit*, *Stand*, *Granta*, *Edinburgh Review* and the *Warwick Review*, in online publications including *Fleeting* and *The View From Here*, and in anthologies and single-author collections.

I have considered hundreds of stories while reading for this volume. During the past year I have come across lots of good work in anthologies arising out of prizes and competitions, such as *Lightship Anthology 2*, *Bristol Short Story Prize Anthology Volume 5* and *Willesden Herald New Short Stories 6*. Good stuff is coming out of universities in magazines and anthologies. *Matter* and *The Mechanics' Institute Review*, from Sheffield Hallam University and Birkbeck College respectively, adopt the same approach as each other, filling their pages with work by a mixture of MA students and guest writers. Postgraduates from the University of Exeter produce *Peninsula*, a blend of new and old work, fiction, journalism and reportage. *Short Fiction*, from Plymouth University, attracts a range of very good writers. The *Warwick Review* continues to publish excellent short fiction, including, in the past year, outstanding stories by Elizabeth Stott, Alison Moore and Charles Boyle.

Stand has been going for more than 60 years and has moved around a bit; these days it's based at the University of Leeds. If I had had a little more space I would have taken Elizabeth Baines's story from issue 198 as well as Adam Lively's from the issue before. Copies of two excellent independent magazines arrived from Scotland – *Edinburgh Review* and *Gutter*; if the fiction in the former just about had the edge, the look of the latter was a cut above. Also beautifully designed are *Structo*, a UK-based independent literary magazine, and *Magpie Magazine*, which celebrates 'the new folk revolution in art, writing and music' (issue five included a poignant short story by Claire Massey).

If, like me, you feel a little niggle at the way *Granta* doesn't tell you what its pieces are – fiction or non-fiction – go on to the website where they do helpfully tell you what's what. *Boat Magazine* is another expensively produced mix of fiction, journalism and photography; issue three included a good story by Lee Rourke about the changing fabric of an east London neighbourhood.

Ambit will hopefully cope with founder-editor Martin Bax's retirement in 2013. The novelist and consultant paediatrician has been at the helm for more than fifty years. Andy Cox has been publishing quality horror, science fiction, slipstream and crime stories for two decades; his TTA Press stable of magazines includes *Black Static*, *Interzone* and *Crimewave*.

Three of the year's most interesting anthologies happened to be metropolitan in flavour. There was photographer Roelof Bakker's *Still* (Negative Press London), in which writers were invited to take inspiration from Bakker's photographs of empty spaces in an abandoned Hornsey Town Hall; *Acquired For Development By . . . : A Hackney Anthology* (Influx Press), edited by Gary Budden and Kit Caless, with stories by Gavin James Bower and Lee Rourke, among others, and cover illustrations by Laura Oldfield Ford; and *Road Stories: New Writing Inspired by Exhibition Road* (Royal Borough of Kensington and Chelsea) edited by Mary Morris and beautifully illustrated with paper sculptures by Mandy Smith, in which the story I was most drawn to was Deborah Levy's 'Black Vodka', which would reappear as the title story of the Man Booker 2012 shortlisted author's collection from And Other Stories and then *again* in Comma's *The BBC International Short Story Award*

2012 in which my favourite original story was Julian Gough's inventive and entertaining 'iHole'.

Simon Van Booy's 'The Menace of Mile End' was a highlight of *Red: The Waterstones Anthology*, published by Waterstones (sic, ie no apostrophe. Insert sad face here) and edited by Cathy Galvin, formerly *Sunday Times Magazine* fiction editor who went on to run the popular and successful Short Story Salon at the Society Club. There was a lot of good original work in *Unthology 3* (Unthank Books) edited by Robin Jones and Ashley Stokes, and some hard choices had to be made. The same was true of *Secret Europe*, a lavishly produced large-format collection by John Howard and Mark Valentine published by Exposition Internationale of Bucharest, and of new collections by David Constantine and Joel Lane, whose *Where Furnaces Burn*, a volume of his weird crime stories from the West Midlands that I had been looking forward to for some time, did not in any way disappoint.

What was disappointing about 2012 was, well, a couple of things really. Firstly, the fact that *Prospect* magazine stopped publishing original stories in its fiction slot, opting for stories extracted from forthcoming collections instead. It's easier for the editor concerned, but it does turn the magazine (with regard to that slot only, of course) from a worthy sponsor of new writing into nothing more than a shop window for publishers. Secondly, the disappearance off my radar of *London Magazine*.

I have been an avid reader and collector of *London Magazine* since I moved to the capital in the early 1980s. It's been around a lot longer, of course, since 1732 in fact. It was the first magazine to which I submitted my own short stories (they were politely returned by the then editor Alan Ross, a true gentleman of publishing). I watched it get picked up by Picador for a while and then get put down again. It went through editors like an underperforming football club goes through managers. Unpaid, I wrote a film column for the magazine for a year, glad of the free copy. Then the current editor, Steven O'Brien, took over and the magazine started to take on a distinct flavour with the appearance on the masthead and contents page of names like Grey Gowrie, Bruce Anderson, Peregrine Worsthorne. There was invariably room for one or more of editor O'Brien's poems. My review copies stopped arriving – a series like *The Best British Short Stories* can't do its job without the willingness of publishers to provide review copies – and my emailed requests went unanswered. I wondered if 'special editorial advisor' Gowrie, who resigned his Cabinet post in 1985 because it was impossible for him to live in central London on the £33,000 salary, had advised cuts. After a number of ignored pleas via a variety of media, I finally heard from an intern that the editor did not 'feel inclined to offer a free subscription'. From the amount of champagne flowing at the magazine's 2012 autumn party (pictures posted online) it doesn't look as if austerity has hit particularly hard. I'm just sorry I missed Gowrie's 17-page poem 'The Andrians', and even sorrier I've not been able to keep up with the magazine's short stories, including, last year, two by Steven O'Brien.

NICHOLAS ROYLE
Manchester
March 2013

THE *Best* {BRITISH} *Short Stories* 2013

ALISON MOORE

THE SMELL OF THE SLAUGHTERHOUSE

RACHEL'S FATHER OPENS the door and looks at her. Seeing her small suitcase, he says, 'Is that it?'

'I'll go back for more,' she says. She will go when Stan's out. If she goes when he's in, he will tell her that he loves her, and she doesn't want to hear it. Or perhaps she won't go back. She could leave it all behind and buy new clothes, new everything.

Stepping inside, she sees that she is treading something into the house. She leaves the offending shoe outside, puts the other one on the shoe rack and hangs up her coat. Her father, closing the door behind her, fetches paper towels and carpet freshener. Then he picks up her suitcase and she follows him through the floral mist to the stairs.

He carries her suitcase up to her room, puts it down on the bed and says, 'I'll leave you to it.'

She packed hastily but has remembered her make-up. She takes her cosmetics case into the bathroom, where she washes her hands and face with her father's soap before reapplying her foundation, covering the bruising.

Back in her bedroom, she undresses, putting her clothes into the laundry basket and choosing something clean from her suitcase. She puts the rest of her things into the drawers and onto hangers. Her room has not changed at all. When she has finished unpacking and has put her empty suitcase under the bed, it is almost as if she has never been away.

She can hear the kettle boiling and crockery chinking in the kitchen.

Downstairs, she finds her father on his way into the dining room with a pot of tea, cups and a packet of lemon sponge fingers on a tray. Putting everything down on the table, he says, 'Shall I be mother?'

Her mother always had a clean shirt waiting for Rachel's father when he got in from work, ready for him to put on after his shower. He smelt heavily of his carbolic soap at teatime.

There was always a cloth on the dining table, and something home-baked. There might be some quiet jazz on the stereo. Her mother would pour the tea and ask about his day. He never really talked about it though. 'Fine,' he would say, or, 'Busy.'

Her mother would say, 'Good,' or, 'It's better to be busy,' and nothing much more would be said.

Rachel, sitting down now at the table and accepting sugar in her tea, remembers how she used to look at her father, at the well-washed hands in which he held his slice of cake and his teacup, and she would think to herself that no one would know he had just come from the abattoir.

Except that the smell of the carbolic soap with which he scrubbed himself daily, and whose reek is on her own skin now, has come to seem to her, over the years, like the smell of the slaughterhouse itself.

ELLIS SHARP

THE WRITER

SWIRLED WITH MORTALITY, entropy, a sense of wasting, the notion of shrinkage was still with him. The day before, he'd stepped from a northbound Bakerloo train at Oxford Circus, crossed to the Victoria Line and seen, at the end of a stump of corridor, a pair of massive eyes, a vast nose, the helium-filled grossness of a bloated mouth. The giant stared directly at him, with eyeballs the size of footballs. In their flinty blackness Doodles noted a second, more striking resemblance, to the pitiless eyes of the pug in Joshua Reynolds' painting of George Selwyn, the necrophiliac MP and Satanist, which had transfixed him just thirty-two minutes earlier. As he moved towards the platform – there was no avoiding the giant, as Doodles had to get to Kings Cross – his recognition of those eyes and shrunken cheekbones was, metre by metre, confirmed. He felt like a mouse in the Jagger villa.

Next day Doodles left the Lido behind, in the care of the local authority, and continued along a rising tarmac pathway. The balconies of an adjacent block of flats displayed plants in pots, ironwork chairs and some sodden towels. Soon he was beyond the flats, the path forked, and he went left, as he had been doing since his late teens.

The path here was narrower. To his right a grassy slope rose gently to a ridge, where a dozen trees crowded together for company. The grass had recently been cut and dead swathes of it lay like tufts of hair on a barber's floor. Death had made the stems curl and become yellowish. On the slope nine ravens stood at a distance of twenty metres from each other. It was as if they had been placed there by a film director who'd graduated with a special interest in surrealism.

The nearest raven cautiously edged a couple of paces away from Doodles as he passed but otherwise maintained its air of dignified alertness. None of the ravens seemed to be looking for worms, or doing anything but stand amid the dying grass, motionless, lost in meditation. The blackness of their plumage seemed lurid and their normal size was magnified fifty per cent. Perhaps it was the effect of the rain, which had been falling with a mild persistence ever since he'd reached the Lido. Doodles' glasses were speckled and distorted by watery blobs.

He stopped and glanced back at London. The gherkin was a dull grey and looked less like a gherkin than a styptic pencil. The financial district was a heap of grey cardboard boxes. Only the Telecom tower had clarity. Its encrustation of pale dishes resembled fungi on a dead trunk. The metaphor made him think of the path beyond the golf club at Seaton.

At the foot of the slope a toy train rattled along the line from Gospel Oak, passing a plum-coloured running track. The rain was much denser to the south and the city was fuzzy and smudged by mistiness.

He turned and went on. Beyond the final raven a grassy track skirted the mown area and went up to the brow of the hill. On the skyline a few trees huddled together for company. Doodles moved on to this pathway, the ground beneath his boots suddenly malleable and springy, yielding to his weight with a low squelch of pleasure. He trudged up to the top, the rain determined to glue his jeans to his kneecaps.

An enigmatic rectangle of concrete came into view. As he

reached it – was it a covering or the base of something which had long ago been removed? – Doodles was enveloped by mist. A squall of rain struck him hard across the cheeks, which made him think of Alice. How her hot temper and fondness for drugs had excited him in the old days! But now he was alone, half a stone heavier, blundering blindly down a hillside, lashed by icy splashes, embraced by a thickening fog, seeing nothing but a patch of thorns. He was starting to feel like a character in *The Pilgrim's Progress* – Mr Wandering Wet-Man. At one point he slipped and almost fell into a narrow ditch concealed by an emerald blanket of wild cress, saved not by Christian fortitude (he had exhausted his quota by his ninth year) but by the thick tread of his boots, size eleven feet, gigantic thighs, and a yoga-friendly sense of balance.

Slithering and skipping, Doodles reached the base of a broad grassy valley. The Diazepam and his momentum bore him giddily as far as the bare, branchless trunk of a strangely uncontoured tree, the smooth surface of which was a uniform chocolate brown. Seizing hold of it to halt his onward movement – the edge of a cliff or a ravine might be just a few metres away in the mist – Doodles was shocked to find himself clinging to cold, greasy metal. As if that human contact triggered synthetic climatic effects, the mist evaporated and Doodles discovered that he was standing underneath some sort of large eight-legged structure. He wondered if it was a drowsy, monstrous spider and he had lately been exposed to a massive dose of radioactivity. That would explain the shrinkage.

It was only when he ran, screaming, towards the nearby lake and momentarily glanced back that he saw what it was. A massive desk with an equally massive high-backed five-spined chair tucked underneath it. Whoever it belonged to – King Kong? – had evidently gone off for a coffee.

Where was everyone? Hampstead Heath was completely empty. Doodles reached the broad tarmac path which passed alongside the lake. Sweating, he ran along it to the next lake and beyond. A muddy gleaming track led up another hill towards woodland. Best to get under cover, he thought, and crossed a tiny bridge coated with chicken wire. Half way up he paused to let a big black shining slug cross. The twin blobs of its antennae swayed from side to side, as if sensing his presence. When it had reached the grass on the far side of the hardened, well-trodden earth Doodles dodged past it and ran on into the wood. Here, vertical strips of lighting were fixed to the trees, joined by loops of finger-thick wiring. Three or four minutes later he saw another, smaller lake. Beyond it was a stage, protected by a helmet-shaped canopy. To his right, stacked deckchairs dripped in a roped-off clearing. Behind them a grey portable toilet leaned at a perilous angle.

Kenwood House came into view, put there by that same surrealist film director. Gravel displaced the tarmac. The magnolia tree was a lush green and nothing at all like the day it had been when he had made Alice laugh by rolling sideways down the slope. He had collided with the metal fence at the bottom, hurting his head and his ribs. A park ranger wearing the insignia of English Heritage ticked him off. Doodles apologised, explaining that he was a Celt and that Alice had run out of money for drugs. The ranger snarled and strode off home to his collection of artefacts from the Weimar Republic. That day the magnolia tree bore an extravagant white, wedding day blossom. Doodles took Alice's hand and led her through the hornbeam tunnel, afterwards presenting her with a photocopy of pages 702 and 703 from a hardback novel where the hero also walks into this same leafy arbour. Doodles passed through and on towards Dr Johnson's summer house, inside which he encouraged Alice to drink from his flask of whisky to ease the shivering. It wasn't there, and only now did he recall that it had been destroyed by fire.

He went on across the lawn to Hepworth's 'Empyrean',

which holds the meaning of life. Alice nodded with a deep understanding. Today it was desolate and deserted and people had scratched their initials on the surface. Doodles, who was six and a half feet tall, felt as if his stomach consisted of a large oval-shaped hole. He went inside the house and looked at the dull Vermeer, which established how much guitars had changed. The incomplete circle behind Rembrandt's shoulder disturbed him, as it always did. Much of the painting seemed fuzzy and dark and out of focus. Doodles remembered it was time for his eye test.

The gallery was empty. Even the attendants had deserted their corner chairs. On the velvet cushion of one a PD James crime thriller lay asleep on its big smug stomach.

The library was sickly with gilt. The enormous bookshelves with their big interminable matching volumes suggested Hollywood's idea of what a private library should be like. A leaflet gave interesting facts. It took three men eight days to fit the mirrors in this temple of kitsch and neo-classical mediocrity. The only object of interest was a stone bust of Homer, formerly the property of Alexander Pope. It looked significantly different to the bust of Homer once belonging to Alexander Pope in the painting which hung over the fireplace.

On the way back everything was the same, except reversed. Doodles paused to let the slug go by. The lakes were windswept and desolate. The rain fell in the alternative slant. The giant's desk and chair were still, like the surrounding landscape, unoccupied.

The ravens had gone. On the way down to the Lido, Doodles met a hooded woman coming the other way who gave him a warm smile. He exchanged it for one many degrees lower.

Returning along Chetwynd Park Road, drenched Doodles felt his mood sag. He was very wet and very cold, and the day seemed as blustery and rainswept as that Sunday when the circus departed. All morning there was a crash and clatter of dismantled scaffolding and folded machinery. The lions groaned in their cages and tyres span amid liquid mud. The next day the blueprint was marked out in the field in circles and rectangles of brown dead grass edged by perforations where pegs had stabbed the earth.

A pretty ending. But no Sunday when a circus departed existed in his memory. Doodles did not wear glasses. He was only five feet four, and losing an inch every year. The train was obviously not a toy and the metaphor was arthritic and lazy. The ravens were there earlier but they were not ravens but rooks. Trees have no emotions and do not crowd together for company. Seeds are spilled but only a few take root. The anthropomorphic tendencies in this story are deplorable. The ground emitting a low squelch of pleasure! Rain with malign intentions against the jeans worn by Doodles! And 'plum coloured' is a meaningless description, since plums are variously coloured – empurpled, green, rouge, blotchy-brown and so on. Ditto 'chocolate coloured'. My favourites in a box are always the white ones. And Doodles did not almost fall into a ditch, for there wasn't one. No wild cress attracted his notice. And there was a mistake made in remembering the library. In fact it took eight men three days to fit those preposterous mirrors.

Between paragraphs twelve and thirteen Doodles went into the coffee bar at Kenwood and ate a hummus and grated carrot wrap, washed down with cappuccino. Giancarlo Neri's installation was not a surprise and was the express reason Doodles went to Hampstead Heath on Wednesday 24 August 2005. There was no mist around the desk and chair and Doodles did not scream. The slug, which was slug-sized, was not there on the way back. It was in fact the day after the Hampstead trip that Doodles went to Tate Britain to see the Joshua Reynolds exhibition, and not thirty-two minutes but several hours later at Oxford Circus that he encountered the hoarding for the new Rolling Stones album. In between he went to the Twining's shop opposite the Royal Courts of Justice and bought six packets of Irish Breakfast, his favourite tea. After that he went to Waterloo station to meet someone who was arriving on the Portsmouth Harbour train. The slope he rolled down was in Scotland. There was no ranger. There was a girl and there were drugs but her name was not Alice and she and Doodles never went to Hampstead. The Diazepam was years ago and back then named Valium. Alice never existed, except in a Victorian classic. But the route mapped out in this story is entirely accurate.

ADAM MAREK

THE STORMCHASERS

IT'S SO WINDY today. My son Jakey and I are at the window watching leylandii bow to each other, and the snails being blown across the patio like sailboats.

We've been watching for fifteen minutes or so when Jakey says, 'I'm scared.'

'Of what?' I ask.

'Of tornadoes.'

'Listen,' I say, 'no tornadoes are coming here. Even if we got in the car right now and drove around all day like the stormchasers on TV, we'd be lucky to find one. Very lucky.'

'But what if we did?'

There is a noise from behind us. We both look at the fireplace. The wind is playing the chimney like a flute.

'Even if we were really lucky and did find one,' I say, 'in England it would be a tiny thing. We don't get the big ones here.'

'An F4?' he asks. We have watched documentaries about tornadoes together since he was a baby. Among six-year-olds, he is an expert.

'No way,' I say. 'An F2, if we were *really* lucky.'

'Big enough to suck up a person?'

He is imagining the tornado like a straw in the sky's mouth, I can see this.

'Nuh-uh,' I say. 'Just big enough to fling a couple of roof tiles about, or knock over some flowerpots, or break a greenhouse to pieces.'

'But what if . . .' he starts.

He is not going to believe me, sitting here in the house with the wind whoo-whooing around our walls like a ghost.

'Go get changed out of your jim-jams,' I say. 'I'll show you that there's nothing to be afraid of.'

While Jakey looks for his shoes, I pack lunch for us in a cotton shoulder bag: for me, chicken-liver pate and apple chutney sandwiches, and a flask of Earl Grey tea; for Jakey, cheese spread sandwiches, a fun-size Twix and two cartons of apple juice.

'All set?' I say when he gets to the bottom of the stairs. He is wearing the bright yellow sou'wester and macintosh that he has finally grown into. I bought them for him before he was born, when he was just in my imagination.

'Uh-huh,' he says.

'We'd better go say goodbye to mum,' I say.

We creep upstairs together, peep around the bedroom door. Mum is still in bed. She has the light out. Yesterday the dentist at the hospital pulled four wisdom teeth from her mouth. She has been in bed for a whole day, and mostly silent.

'Where are you going?' she says. Even her voice sounds wounded.

'We're going tornado chasing,' Jakey says.

'We won't be long,' I say. 'Can I get you anything?'

'No.'

'Are you feeling okay?' Jakey asks.

She pulls the duvet over her head. 'Just go away,' she says.

We drive.

'It feels good to be out, doesn't it?' I say. 'Seen any tornadoes yet?'

Jakey looks around. He says nothing.

The bendy roads between the hedgerows are full of fallen branches so I go slow. We live in the countryside, a little house all on its own. In the summer, from the air, our plot is a dark green triangle in the middle of a bright yellow sea of rapeseed. I have seen it from the air, in a microlight. The photograph I took is in our bathroom. I stare at it every time I pee.

'Where shall we go?' I say. 'If we were proper stormchasers, Jakey, we'd have a Doppler radar and a laptop so we could find the tornadic part of the storm.'

'We *are* real stormchasers,' he says.

I'm watching the road carefully but I can see his pout from the corner of my eye.

'You're right,' I say. 'But we don't have Doppler, so we'll have to rely on our instincts. You take a look at the sky and tell me where you think the tornadoes will touch down.'

Jakey presses the window button till the window is open the whole way. He sticks his head out. I slow the car and move into the middle of the road so he doesn't get hit by the sticky-out branches that the hedge-mower has missed. I'm going slow enough that I can watch Jakey. He is looking up into the sky, holding the door frame with both hands. The wind is throwing his shaggy hair all around his head. His hair is cornfield-blond, the same as mine. His mum's is almost black. 'Yet another thing he got from you, not me,' she sometimes says.

'That way,' he says, pointing north-east.

When we get to the motorway, the car is hard to control. The wind bullies our left-hand side. The windscreen wipers are overwhelmed with this much rain. We feel enclosed, in the car.

We are like a head in a hood. Jakey gets to choose the radio station. He chooses pop music. He sings along.

'How do you know the words to all these songs?' I ask.

'Mum listens to this radio station,' he says.

I do not like pop music, but I do like to hear Jakey sing.

We've been driving for twenty minutes, when ahead we see a smudge of yellow on the horizon. The rain is thinning. The cars coming towards us on the other side of the motorway have their lights off. In the rear-view mirror is a procession of lit headlamps, bright against the bruise-black sky.

'We should turn around,' I say.

'No. It's this way,' Jakey says.

'Are you sure?'

'Uh-huh.'

We reach sunlight. The wet tarmac around us is steaming.

'Are you sure the tornadoes are this way, Jakey?'

'No.'

'Shall we turn around?'

It looks like the end of the world back the way we came. Within the wall of cloud, there's a heck of a light show.

'Okay,' Jakey says.

I come off the motorway and go round the roundabout three times – our game when Mum's not in the car. Jakey giggles, pinned to the door by physics.

We go back the way we came. I break the speed limit now because the storm is running away from us. We eat our lunches from our laps while we drive.

'If you're scared of tornadoes,' I say, 'why do you want to see one so badly?'

Jakey shrugs, finishing his apple juice. It gurgles at the bottom of the carton.

'Well, I told you we'd be very lucky to see one. Stormchasers drive thousands of miles to find them, drive around for weeks sometimes.'

'How far have we driven?'

'About 80 miles. Shall we go home now? Mum'll be wondering where we are.'

'Yes,' he says.

The sun follows us back. We lead it all the way to our front gates. Jakey picks up handfuls of the leaves that are heaped against our porch and drops them again. I put Jakey's lunch rubbish in the cotton bag before I get out. I open the front door and we both go inside.

'We're home!' I call, wiping my feet.

No answer.

I tiptoe upstairs. Our bed is empty.

'Dad!' Jakey calls out.

I run downstairs.

In the living room, the coffee table is on its side against the wall. One of its legs is broken off. The TV is face down on the carpet. The mantelpiece above the fireplace is bare. All the photos and pinecones and holiday souvenirs are on the floor. Some are smashed on the slate tiles in front of the wood burner. On the walls, the pictures are all at angles. Jakey's toys are tipped from his box.

In the middle of it all, sitting on the floor with her arms round her legs, and her forehead on her knees, is mummy. Her knuckles are bloody.

Jakey moves towards her. I hold him back with my hand.

'Don't. There's glass,' I say. 'You okay, mummy? Did you see it, the tornado? When it came through?'

No answer. No movement.

Only she and I know that the story about the dentist was a terrible lie.

JACKIE KAY

MRS VADNIE MARLENE SEVLON

ON THE WAY home from a long and final day in Sunnyside Home for the Elderly, Mrs Vadnie Marlene Sevlon was relieved to notice a little breeze. Much better than yesterday when the weather was close, so close she felt the low pressure in the air. As long as there is a little breeze, a person can cope with most things – even if she is in the wrong place. It's the days when there is no breeze at all when Vadnie is convinced she made a mistake. But it wasn't like there ever seemed much choice. It wasn't like she could just take her pick. Only people with money have choice; only rich people can take their pick; everyone else must stumble from pillar to post, from hope to promise, and believe in luck and God, or maybe just God, or maybe just luck, depending on the day and the breeze. Vadnie Marlene Sevlon often said her own name, her whole name, to herself when she was alone. Perhaps because it reminded her of back home, her mother shouting *Vadnie Marlene Sevlon, come and get your dinner*, or maybe because it made her feel less lonely or maybe even just to remind herself of who she was. Time for you to get up, Vadnie Marlene Sevlon, she would say in the morning; bed for you now, Vadnie Marlene Sevlon, she would say at night. And in between the morning and the night sometimes not a single living soul said her name out loud.

Vadnie walked past the College for Boys, past the Brondesbury Park Rail Station and the Islamia Primary School, past Willesden Lane Cemetery where sometimes if she had a little time on her hands she would sit on a bench and contemplate the differences between the living and the dead. She liked to read the gravestones and imagine the lives of the fascinating names she read, and work out the ages, practising her mental arithmetic. Some people find graveyards gloomy, but not Vadnie Marlene; she felt as if she was being kept company by the peaceful dead. There was an atmosphere in Willesden Lane Cemetery that you never found in Kilburn High Street or at work or even at home. Intense contemplation! Vadnie sometimes envisaged her own headstone, though she knew nobody in her family could afford one, and anyway they wouldn't want her buried in England, and anyway she was too young to be thinking such thoughts. (She was fifty-two, hardly a spring chicken, but then not likely to be at death's door any time soon, please God. Her father was dead long time back now, but her mother was still around and living in Darling Spring, Jamaica, with three of her sisters who all wanted Vadnie to come back home. 'South of here is Grateful Hill, South West, Lucky Valley, further south then, Prospect,' her mother used to say often, 'I'm hoping our prospects improve soon.') But even so her mind would wander off, as it often did, to imagining her own death, and she'd envisage her whole name and her dates and the inscription *beloved daughter of Gladstone and Hyacinth Sevlon, Rest in Peace, Darling.* It wasn't perhaps what people usually did in their lunch hours, dream up their own headstones, but Vadnie found it quite entertaining and it passed away the time. Should it say *passed away* or should it say *fell asleep*, what should the exact wording be? She continued down Salusbury Road, stopped to buy a new plug in the

DIY shop and a new packet of fuses, past the artisan bakery, where the bread and cakes looked lovely, like little works of art, the beauty of those breads, some so threaded they looked like fancy hair-dos, or wiring, but cost a small fortune, so she only ever looked in the window; past a fancy florist where they even had birds of paradise, which looked out of place, but cost a small fortune so she only ever went in to the florist's to take a deep sniff; past Queen's Park Underground Station and right into Kilburn Lane, down Fifth Avenue, which always made Vadnie think of New York, where she might have gone for her contemplation, *Central Park*, watching people skateboard, rollerblade, jog, meditate, dance and all the things she heard say people do in Central Park from her cousin Eldece who went over there fifteen years ago and sometimes wrote a letter with all her news. Eldece was maybe the lucky one. But the strange thing about life was that you could only live the one of them; you couldn't live the other one, the one where you went to New York instead of London, and then compare and contrast. You couldn't compare the life you had with the life you might have had though sometimes Vadnie Marlene Sevlon would have liked to be able to shout *Stop* and after the requisite minutes *Start*, and then catch the other life, live it for a bit, and if it was not as agreeable as the one in her imagination, well then she'd be able to return to the old life and appreciate it better by simply shouting *Stop* and *Start* again. As Vadnie turned into her own street, Oliphant Street, she wondered if it was luck or fate or God that made the decisions in your life. Or was it just a moment plucked from the ordinary that made you stick with mistakes already made? For instance, once, years ago, on the telephone, a man who was going to be coming to fix her electric sockets said, 'Is you Miss or Mrs?' And Vadnie answered Mrs. That was twenty years ago, when she was thirty, and was still thinking that the right man might come along. He never did but Vadnie kept the Mrs anyway. She put Mrs on her bank cards and Mrs on anything she had to sign. Mrs on her direct debits and Mrs on her television licence, Mrs on her water bill and Mrs on her gas and electric. It was Mrs Vadnie Sevlon, and she felt she got more respect that way. Strange thing was, after a number of years, she believed it herself. She was no longer surprised at the amount of post that arrived with her whole name on it. The Mrs by then didn't give her the thrill of the early days; she took it quite for granted. So might she look back on the electric man and call that fate or luck or God? Did God want her to call herself Mrs to keep herself safe from men of disrepute? When people asked her what her husband did, she would tell them he was an electrician. She would picture him vividly, combining features of the electrician with the features of a man she once sat next to on a bus to the Lake District. She made a kind of composite husband out of the two, took the hair from one and gave it to the other so he wasn't balding, just receding, took two inches of height from one and gave it to her husband, made his skin a rich dark brown. Her husband had lovely neat nails which you might not expect for an electrician. 'Oh, he works long hours; he's an electrician you see. You have to be very well qualified to be an electrician, you know. You have to know your wires, your blue and brown and black and yellow. And you need to know that blue used to be neutral, but black also used to be neutral,' Vadnie would say, whenever she got a chance, to whoever would listen, even strangers, knowledgeably quoting the most recent electrician who stood explaining his job to her for some time on the last visit to Oliphant Street. Vadnie didn't quite know what it was that made boiler men and electricity men and plumbing men always like to explain to her the exact ins and outs of what they were doing in a supremely technical way, but when an electrician came around, Vadnie listened intently. (In fact, she had found herself sometimes putting in extra plugs she didn't exactly need and could ill afford, just to be sure she was up to date.) She had to have her husband keep up with the changing times and colour codes, she couldn't have him caught short, her husband, dear Preston, Preston Sherwin Audley Sevlon; she felt such a tenderness for him. Preston: a quiet man, a man of few words, but kind deeds, whose parents were also from Jamaica but had come to England once and worked in Preston before returning to Montego Bay – well this was the story Vadnie first of all made up and later believed. When she got home from work, Preston would say, 'Put your feet up, Mrs Sevlon, and I'll make you a cup of tea.' He never raised his voice or his hand to her. He was the kind of man that is a father to daughters rather than sons, a gentle kind man, intense and protective. And of course their daughters, Ladyblossom, Marsha and Grace, were all daddy's girls. If you'd had a son, Preston would say, he would have been a mummy's boy. What would we have called a son? she heard herself asking Preston. A name after an English place, he'd say, like me, chuckling, enjoying himself, Carlisle or Kendal or Lancaster. I couldn't call a little boy Lancaster, she'd find herself saying out loud in the kitchen – then startle herself with his absence. Was it luck that got her the job as a care home orderly at Sunnyside Home for the Elderly? Or was she being deliberately led down the wrong path? It was only two days a week but it seemed like a beginning in the beginning. And she well remembered the first day all that time ago, why, it must be fifteen years at least, walking down the driveway and glimpsing the garden with the bench, the table with the green umbrella, thinking the place was really something quite, quite special. The grounds were grand and made her feel she was definitely in England. They were a people that knew how to make a garden, the English! And during the first few weeks Vadnie would eat her Coronation chicken sandwich in the palatial garden with the blossom on the trees and the green grass under her feet and feel almost content; at least, the worry about money and the future would lift and she would be in the unusual position of just being able to sit and eat her sandwich and watch the birds flit about in the trees. She always kept her eye out for a Barbuda warbler even though she didn't think they ever came to this country. But if birds of paradise could be in the florist then Barbuda warblers could be in the garden. It would have lifted her heart to see a bird from back home in the garden of Sunnyside Home for the Elderly. She didn't much like the two women who ran Sunnyside, and they didn't get any better over time. For a start they had no sense of humour, which was quite a problem. Vadnie had never realised how big a problem this could be until she first ran into the two sad Sunnyside women. All the good conversation has to have a little light-ness! Well, the first thing Vadnie said to the matron was, 'The garden is quite something. What lovely borders! You do all the weeding yourself?' (Of course she was joking, and was going to go on to mention the beautiful garden design, but the matron – she didn't get it.) She replied seriously, snooty-like, 'No, no. We have a gardener.' Just like that. And Vadnie nodded, undaunted, and said, 'Handsome man is he, this gardener? About my age do you think?' Matron stared and said, 'He's Irish,' as if that might be something that would put Vadnie off. 'And he's in his seventies.' That would be the clincher, then. So after that Vadnie never joked with Matron, which meant there was no basis for conversation; there was only a way of receiving instructions. And the head nurse was even worse. She had something nasty about her, that woman, and no mistake. She was always picking fault. She'd say to Vadnie, 'Did you *say* you had washed the kitchen floor?' when the floor was gleaming, gleaming, so shiny Vadnie could see her face in it, which was the test her mother had given her when she was a little girl. She would say, *Have you polished so bright you can see your reflection?* Whenever Vadnie did see her reflection in some domestic surface, it never looked like her, and she'd have to pause for a minute and say, *Is that me, is that really me?* Sometimes she loomed in things. She appeared all out of proportion.

Still it is not an absolute necessity to get on with the people you work for, especially not when they are your boss. When you do get on with them, they can let you down even more. Vadnie remembered the woman she cleaned for in St Elizabeth in Jamaica saying, 'Very sorry, Vads, but you're no longer needed. You did such an excellent job and have been like family to us, but . . . ' And what was the real reason? The details of the thing had gone, but the hurt was still there. That was the interesting thing about hurt. All the vocabulary can go, all the words said and heard, and yet the pain persists in your heart, slow and heavy. The worst hurts were wordless, or at least they became wordless. A lot of the old people in Sunnyside Home for the Elderly didn't speak, or if they did speak they didn't make that much sense. They seemed in their own world, a lost world, a vanquished world. They didn't have many places like this back home. The family took the elderly in and that was that. Imagine the planning: building these big houses to incarcerate all the old mummies and daddies, imagine the spreadsheets and architectural blueprints, to hide away all the old grandparents. Imagine inventing these places for them. Even if Sunnyside did have a nice garden, it was still a kind of hell. All of the grandmas and grandpas lined up to look out of the window! They were never allowed out to take a little stroll. Once Vadnie asked Matron if she could take a stroll with one of the women, Margaret, and Matron said, We are not insured to allow them to walk about in the garden. Would you pay if she fell over? Would you pay all the damages? Something like that. Vadnie said, Yes, it'll be fine, she won't fall over, she is quite steady on her feet. But Matron shook her head and said, So you think I'm paying you to go strolling around the garden? You must think I was born yesterday. Vadnie stopped to consider this seriously for a moment, the idea that the matron could be born yesterday and then grow in such a short space of time into such a nasty old woman. Not possible! Nastiness needs time to build up.

Today the morning had started with Vadnie saying to herself, Time to get up, Vadnie Marlene Sevlon. Preston was up and out and had not brought her the usual cup of hot tea. The girls had already grown up and left home. Grace was the first in the family at university. Sometimes, she'd find herself doing a big shop and telling people the family was coming home, that's why her trolley was suddenly loaded. Today nobody was there and nobody was coming home and she felt suddenly tired. Odd times at the Sunnyside Home for the Elderly, she'd found herself having to take a ten-pound note or two to help her get by because they didn't pay her enough and because the old people were not going anywhere anyway and none of them would miss it and because she was the only one in the place who was kind so deserved it and because she tried to do good things with it, often buying them little treats, and sometimes even buying them clothes. But today the day didn't feel right from the word go. When she arrived in Sunnyside, Margaret, her favourite of the old people and the most with-it and the one who took the most interest in Preston and the girls, implored her to buy her a cherry red cardigan. She was in some distress. 'Would you manage to buy me a red cardigan,' she asked, her voice shrill, anxious. 'I'll try my best,' Vadnie found herself saying. 'Tell me your size.' And Margaret looked happy, happy as she'd ever seen her. She was sure that the matron and the other one didn't treat them well; Vadnie thought they might even be abusive but she never saw anything with her own eyes. Recently, though, she had made heavy hints about the authorities, and she had sat at home glued to a documentary about a whistleblower. (She had never heard the term before.) 'I might blow the whistle,' Vadnie had thought to herself. 'Tell me,' Vadnie said to Margaret quietly, 'won't you tell me if they ever lay a finger on you?' Maybe one of them overheard; Vadnie didn't know how it had all started. But at the end of the day that had started strangely, Vadnie found herself dismissed. After twenty years: dismissed. And the thing that distressed her most was that she wouldn't be able to return with Margaret's cherry red cardigan. She wouldn't be able to tell Margaret how Preston was, how Ladyblossom, Grace and Marsha were doing. They might as well all be dead.

On the way home Vadnie felt the breeze on her face and the strange feeling turning into Oliphant Street that violence was in the air. She walked slowly, heavily. She had a tight feeling across her chest. She was sweating. She stopped in the DIY shop and bought a new plug and a new packet of fuses. 'My husband used to be an electrician,' she told the woman, 'yet could I get him to fix a plug?' The woman in the shop laughed. 'Mine is a carpenter – ditto!' She paused. 'You said "used to",' the woman said. Vadnie nodded slowly, 'Yes, he passed away a few weeks ago. He's buried up the road there in Willesden Cemetery.' 'Oh, I'm sorry,' the woman said. Mrs Vadnie Marlene Sevlon dabbed at the sudden tears falling down her face. 'He was a good man, a terribly good man,' she said.

ROSS RAISIN

WHEN YOU GROW INTO YOURSELF

A FEW DRIVERS had slowed to look up at the side of the coach as it circled the roundabout. Along one stretch of its window, near the back, three pairs of white buttocks were pressed against the glass like a row of film-packed chicken breasts. As the coach lurched off the roundabout one of these pairs of buttocks briefly disappeared, before returning emphatically to its place alongside the others.

Inside the coach Tom sat alone beside his kitbag, looking across the aisle at the hysterical gurning faces of the three mooners.

The middle one had dropped his trousers to his ankles, his cock bobbing stupidly with the motion of the vehicle as it overtook a caravan on to the dual carriageway. Tom turned away, embarrassed, glad that the short journey was nearly over.

The coach was on its way to a budget hotel on the outskirts of town, an away-match policy now insisted upon by the chairman in the aftermath of the opening weekend of the season. Tom had not been at the club then. He had signed a few weeks later, shortly after being let go by his boyhood club in a brief and tearful meeting with the new manager. The memory of that afternoon was still difficult to think about. All of the second-year apprentices lined up in the corridor among the new man's cardboard boxes and whiteboards; the office and its stale stink of the old manager's cigarettes. Tom had stood by the door as the manager perched on his desk, which was empty except for a scribbled piece of paper and a scratched glass case with a blue cap inside it.

'You're a good lad, Tommy. Your parents should be proud of you. No question you'll find a club. You're going to be some player, when you grow into yourself.'

Tom found out afterwards that he'd said the exact same thing to all of them, except the two he'd kept on. Eight lads he had progressed through all the youth levels with, all hoping now for another club to phone them as they thumbed through the jobs pages or took on work at the recruitment agency, the shopping centre, the multiplex, waiting to grow into themselves. Unlike most of them, though, Tom did find a club. A small town down south, near the coast. The chairman phoned up himself, one morning, and arranged for him to stay in a hotel for the night so that he could come down and talk to them.

'Who?' his sister had said when he told his family. 'League what?'

'Two. They came up from the Blue Square last year. Chairman says they've got some money behind them.'

His sister told him well done and then went upstairs to ring her friends and tell them the news.

The three backsides had returned to their seats. They were still laughing. One of them, scanning round to see if anybody was still watching them, caught Tom's eye, and Tom gave him a dumb grin before turning to look out of the window. Cars moved past them in the other lane. Out of some, the blue-

and-yellow scarf of that day's opposition flapped and spanked against back windows, and one or two drivers honked their horns as they overtook the coach.

The match had begun promisingly. It was his first start for the team, and the sick cramping feeling of the changing room soon left him as he became quickly involved in the game. In one early muscular exchange, as possession swapped repeatedly from one side to the other, the ball spilled out to him on the wing and he ran instantly at the fullback, who, stumbling, tripped, ballooning the ball out over their falling bodies for a corner. A short way into the half, however, a bungle between the two central defenders – who were sat now in the seats in front of Tom watching *Total Wipeout* on a laptop – resulted in a goal for the home side. After that the confidence went from the team. They lost 3-1. In the miserable sweaty fug of the changing room afterwards the manager called them a bunch of soft fucking faggots, and when one of the younger players giggled, the manager stepped forwards and kicked him in the leg.

The coach had left the dual carriageway and was now moving slowly down a superstore-lined arterial road, coming to a halt at traffic lights. A group of home supporters stood outside a pub, smoking. It took a moment for any of them to notice the coach, and when one of them did he seemed unsure what to do, watching it anxiously until a couple of the others followed his stare and started immediately into a frenzy of hand gestures. At his old club, the coach had tinted windows – even the reserve-team coach. In this league, though, the supporters were always in your face. They came up to you in the street and at the supermarket; and inside the small, tight, windswept grounds where they stood grimacing in huddles along the terracing, individual faces and voices were already recognisable to him. The lights changed, and he gave a final glance at the group, rhythmically fist-pumping now in an ecstasy of abuse as the coach began to pull away in the direction of the hotel.

He was rooming with Chris Balbriggan – a situation Balbriggan seemed none too happy with, judging by the way he threw his bag onto the bed by the window, turned the television on too loud and pounded gruntingly at the window for a couple of minutes before accepting finally that it was not designed to open. He stayed there staring out of it instead, occasionally giving a small shake of his head, at his misfortune, or at the flat-roofed view of the neighbouring retail estate. Balbriggan, Yates and Frank Foley, the goalkeeper, were no longer allowed to stay with one another, in any combination, and had all been paired with younger or newer members of the squad.

Although they were banned from room-sharing, the manager did not seem to mind those three keeping company on the nights out after matches. In fact, they were the players that the manager himself kept to, and they formed a boisterous circle near the bar counter of the first place the team went into, while the other players piled into a large sticky red booth or went in pairs around the floor jokingly strong-arming their way into groups of girls.

There was nowhere left to sit in the booth so Tom stood on the outside with the other young players – most of whom had come through the youth team and stuck together – smiling and gravely trying to hear what was being said above the music. Sat immediately below him, Gavin Easter, the right back, was telling a story. Tom kept his eyes on the top of his head, trying, in case anybody should glance at him, to look coolly amused. He could see the raw greased scalp through Easter's stiff clumping hair. He couldn't hear a word. When the story was finished, and the others laughed, Easter leaned back, obviously unaware of Tom stood right behind him because when his shoulder touched Tom's thigh he twisted to look up, and smiled. In a voice that was quiet enough it was probably meant just for him, he said: 'Christ, Tom, if I'd got that close to their lad today maybe we wouldn't have got thumped so badly.' In that moment, Tom felt so grateful that he was almost moved to grip him by the shoulder and say something funny in reply.

He went to the toilet instead. On his way back, in order to avoid being bought a drink, he moved to the bar to buy one for himself. He did not notice, until he got served, that he was wedged up against the back of Frank Foley. Foley was talking to a tall girl with smooth pale shoulders, stood beside him, and each time he leaned in to speak to her his large backside butted against Tom's waist.

The girl was frowning.

'What?'

There was another press of the backside and she nodded, looking out at the room briefly, before turning back to Foley.

'Sorry, love, I've never heard of you.'

She moved to collect three tall glasses of dark liquid and jostled her way out from the bar. Foley stayed where he was, with one arm rested on the counter, looking at his pint. When Tom got out from the bar he was still there, unmoving, the same expression on his face as two thousand other people had already seen three times earlier that day.

Balbriggan did not come back to the room all night, as far as Tom was aware. Tom knew that Balbriggan had returned to the hotel, from the nightclub they'd ended up at, because he was among the mob in the cafe-bar singing and wrestling and drinking from the bottle of rum that somebody had taken from behind the mangled bar shutters.

Tom stayed for about half an hour before going up to bed. He fell asleep immediately, and deeply, before waking just after four with a stiffness in both legs and his face damp with sweat. From the flat glare of a security light outside the window he could see the kitbag still on top of the other bed. He stared at it for a while as he thought back on the day, the match, the night – and a familiar unease came over him that made him close his eyes. His eyelids felt heavy, gummy with perspiration. He became aware of a faint sobbing noise out in the corridor. He kept his eyes closed, trying to shut it out – the noise, the uneasy feeling, the security light.

What got him out of bed in the end was not so much care or curiosity but the creeping anxious thought that if he stayed there listening for much longer then he might begin to cry himself.

He saw immediately where the noise was coming from. At the end of the corridor, in a leggy heap against the wall, beside a fire extinguisher, a young girl was slumped forward with her forehead resting against her knee. He moved towards her. There was the smell of vomit, and a dark tidemark on her shin and calf where it had clung and spiralled down her leg like a chocolate fountain. She was still sobbing quietly but did not look up at him as he kneeled in front of her. She did not respond even as he positioned one arm under her armpits, the other under the tacky back of one knee, then the other, and lifted her up. In the brightness of the corridor lighting, with her eye make-up bleeding and a small pink rash on one of her temples, she looked to him very young, younger even than his sister.

'It's OK,' he whispered. 'It's OK.'

He carried her into the room and kicked Balbriggan's bag off the bed before laying her down and gently arranging the covers over her.

She was still asleep in the exact same position when Balbriggan came into the room when it was light outside. He leaned over Tom's bed gigglingly and slapped him on the cheeks a few times until he was fully awake. As Balbriggan left the room, looking from Tom to the girl and smirking, an unstoppable sensation of pride flared briefly inside him, that turned almost immediately to guilt and stayed with him as he got up, showered and woke the girl – who moved silently into the bathroom to wash her face and leg before letting herself out into the corridor.

When he got to the ground floor to join the squad, she was nowhere to be seen. He didn't ask after her, and he didn't say anything about what had happened to any of the others. He kept to himself – as they filed out of the hotel to the mournful sound of lobby music and the tired, unhappy glances of reception staff – noticing, as he went through the doors, the milky sap in the yucca plant, bent and lolling next to the entrance where the two central defenders had struggled about on top of each other the night before.

The following Saturday he was on the bench. Late in the match, with the team 2–0 down, the manager sent him on, and in his eagerness to show his worth Tom raced into a tackle on the fullback that left him with a badly bruised foot. The injury kept him out of the next two matches. By the time the foot had healed, the manager – with the team in the relegation zone two months into the season – had brought in three loan players, one of them an out-and-out rightwinger, the same side as Tom. On the afternoon of Tom's return to training, the manager approached him during the warm-down to say that he would not be in the next away-match squad.

He spent the evening of the match in his digs, occasionally checking the score on his laptop. He watched television, spoke briefly on the phone to his family and ate a takeaway, a pizza. His dad wanted to come down and help him find a flat of his own to rent. It was getting silly now, his dad said. When Tom signed, the chairman told them that the club would help with finding a place for him, and in the meantime the chairman had one or two small flats of his own that new players could stay in until they got fixed up. As yet, nobody had spoken to him about moving and, as he told his dad on the phone, this didn't feel like the right time to go to the manager asking for help. His dad came down the following week. He had arranged a couple of days off work. They went for a drink, and a meal, and the next day found a studio flat in a new apartment block near the town centre where, they agreed, he would be more in the thick of things. He was proud of him, his dad said. He was doing well, adjusting, considering his age.

They went to a match together, which ended in the first victory of the season. They sat in the main stand. Tom didn't tell him that he had bought their tickets. His dad said that the way this manager liked to play didn't suit his game; it was big-man hoofball and he would need to be patient, roll his sleeves up.

After his dad left, and until the new place was ready, he carried on as before: driving to the training ground in the morning, returning to his digs in the late afternoon. A few times after training and the canteen he went with the other players to the pub across the road where they filled the hours with pool and drinking games and the afternoon races; or sometimes he would drive the short distance to the coast, to one or other of the small resorts there, and walk along the seafronts and beaches. On one of these afternoons there were three boys of about his own age sitting on a bench along a promenade, who stopped their conversation to look up at him as he walked past. When he was a short way further on one of them shouted something, but it got lost in the wind and the movement of the ocean.

Following an especially cheerless defeat the manager called them all in for training the next morning, even though this would normally be a rest day. He was in an unusually threatening mood. In bitter silence they strained and hobbled for lap after lap around the pitches until he was done with them. As the squad began dragging back to the changing rooms, Tom asked the reserve goalkeeper, Hoyle, if he fancied staying behind to practise a few crosses. It wasn't to impress the manager – even though that was of course what the other players would think – but because of the guilty, lonely feeling he had been left with since his dad left. Be patient. Roll your sleeves up. Besides which, the manager always strode away immediately on calling an end to the session, still in his tracksuit, to go and see to his van-hire company.

They practised crossing and catching together for about half an hour, until Hoyle said he was going in. Tom told him he might stay out a bit longer, practise a few drills. Hoyle laughed. 'You're not in the Premiership now, mate. That lot will be in the pub in ten minutes.'

He spaced out half a dozen cones along the right-hand side of the pitch and emptied a bag of balls by the cone furthest from the goal. Then he repeated a shuttle: dribbling around each cone until he reached the dead-ball line, looked up and swung a cross in, aiming each time for the same spot at the near post. He did this until all of the balls were scattered over the neighbouring pitch, where the groundsman had been driving up and down, mowing the grass.

This groundsman now got off his mower and started to jog about, fetching and kicking the balls back to him. Tom, embarrassed, ran to collect the balls himself, but as he got closer he saw that the groundsman was in fact enjoying himself, smiling, and kicking each ball with deliberate aim towards the goal. He was still at it when Tom reached the join of the two pitches, where he stood and watched him kick the rest of the balls. When they were all returned, many of them into the net, the man looked up at him.

'Don't suppose you want to try a few penalties against me, do you?'

He was the younger of the two groundsmen, probably in his early twenties – the older one was in charge of the stadium pitch – and as Tom fired balls at him from the penalty spot he began to wonder if he had been a footballer himself. He was agile, even in his heavy boots and canvas trousers, gleefully diving and saving three of the penalties with the leathery palms of his gardening gloves. Maybe he had been with the club's youth team; one of those who didn't make the cut.

When the balls were finished Tom walked towards him.

'You're good, you know.'

The man was sweating, and wiped a long muddy smear over his broad forehead with the back of a glove. 'Obviously not been taking tips off you lot then, have I?'

He grinned, then started walking back to his mower, as Tom collected the balls and the cones and went to change.

The other players, including Hoyle, had all left, so he took his time showering and changing, enjoying the quiet echo of his studs on the concrete floor and the still-steamy warmth of the shower room, smiling occasionally at the thought of that impromptu penalty session. Afterwards, as he gathered his things, he stared ahead at the pool of shower water struggling around the drain. The thought of driving, of empty windswept beaches, of his bare room in the chairman's flat – his kitbag suddenly felt like a heavy weight in his hand and he sat down, watching as the last of the water eddied and choked down the hole.

He came out onto the pitches and listened for the sound of the mower, but all he could hear was the noise of cars in the distance beyond the fencing and scrubland. On the other side of the four pitches from the road was the small graffitied outbuilding where the groundskeeping equipment was kept, and he made towards this now, trying to ignore the exposed, self-conscious sensation as he walked across the empty expanse of reeking cut grass.

He could see the man through the doorway, carefully pouring the last of one pot of white paint into another on top of a trestle table. Before Tom reached the building he looked round in surprise and, Tom thought, a little amusement.

'What, more penalties?'

The man looked down again and shook the last of the paint into the pot. Tom stood in the doorway. He knew he should say something but he didn't know what that should be. The man did not seem bothered that he was standing there in his doorway watching him work. On the walls, among mounted rakes and shelves of canisters and paint and sprinklers, there were old team posters and a long dirty club scarf that had been nailed up, flecked with paint. Somehow the sight of these things filled Tom with a faint sadness. He watched the man press lids onto the paint pots and move towards the dustbin by the door with the empty pot.

He was about to open the dustbin when Tom reached forward nervously to clasp him on the arm. The man looked at him. Tom let his hand fall to his side and looked down, ashamed, unsure what to say, at the paint pot still in the man's hand, his heavy boots, and his own trainers, now stained with green. He was conscious of how clean he was this close up to the man's work clothes, marked with mud, grass, paint. Tom dared not look up. He listened to the dim thrum of the road. After a few seconds the man turned and Tom watched his back as he moved away, hearing then the unbearable clunk of the paint pot being put down onto the table.

Tom turned to look out of the doorway at the wide abandoned field and he felt the warmth of the man against him. The slow, gradual press of his hands on Tom's sides. Tom stepped forward, pulling himself gently away. Then he turned and looked right at him, at his large doleful face, and he was filled with a sudden glorious sense of risk as the man stood there, waiting for him.

The man was in some pain at first. Tom stopped, not knowing what to do. This had happened the other time, a couple of years ago – neither of them then had been sure how to go on and so they hadn't, trying instead other things, frustrated.

After a moment though, of calmly guiding Tom's hand and then moving it aside, the man indicated for him to continue.

Later, he would remember the smell of paint, and petrol, in the man's hair; the grass cuttings caught there, gradually working themselves loose.

There was no training the next morning because of the weekend's match, so he spent the day moving into his new flat. There was not a lot to move. By midday, he had driven all of his things over from the other place and put them in: his clothes, his stereo, his family's old pots and pans, his posters of his boyhood club. He spent the afternoon arranging these things, with a growing sick jittery sense of how permanent it felt. The thought of the future filled him with anxiety as he moved about the small clean flat and folded his clothes into the wardrobe, sorted the television reception, tacked his posters onto the bedroom walls, then removed them and put them up in the corridor.

He needed to phone his dad and tell him he was in, but he couldn't.

On the afternoon of Saturday's match he went to the players' bar with the other uninvolved members of the first-team squad. He was the only player to watch the match. He stepped out of the bar into the tiny walled-off area at the top of the main stand and sat drinking alone, following absently as the team laboured to a one-all draw, the muffled noise through the glass behind him of Chris Yates and Frank Foley arguing, on and off, all through the match.

He had forgotten to check his route from the flat before he left and got lost around the edge of town, arriving at the training ground over half an hour late. The squad had already begun a keepball routine when the manager, his arms folded, feet planted apart, saw him running towards them.

'Three full circuits, dickhead. Go.'

He started immediately into a fast pace, running in the other direction from the outbuilding, and by the time he had been going only a few minutes, and he heard distantly behind him the sound of the mower starting up, his breath was already coming thickly and his heart thumping. He felt his legs and his chest tighten as he ran faster still – without caring how it would look to the manager and the players – not allowing himself to look round until he had reached the turn at the road side of the pitches.

He saw the small figure on top of the mower as it moved slowly down the side of the furthest pitch and, even from that distance, he knew that it was the other groundsman.

He completed the three circuits and rejoined the others, careful to keep his head down and join fiercely into the training routine, in case any of them might look at his face.

He trained on each of the following days with an intensity that caused him, by the end of the week, to be the object of frequent bruising challenges, all of which went overlooked by the manager and his assistant, surprised and pleased as they were at the sudden unexpected competitiveness brought about by their coaching.

His relations with the other players were not helped either by his insistence on staying behind after the session to train alone, sprinting and sweating, watching, worrying, constantly wondering why – had the two groundsmen swapped roles, or was it something else?

The sour smell of the cut grass, as he limped cramping back to the changing rooms, was almost overpowering.

After two weeks of furious training the manager called him into his office.

'Son, this is what I'd wanted to see when I signed you.'

He was being put back in the first-team squad, the manager told him smugly.

On Tuesday night he was on the bench for a home match. He spent all of it warming up along the touchline, running up and down the side of the pitch, trying to ignore the occasional shouts from the bored, unhappy supporters in the main stand.

Even as the match came towards the end of injury time, and he had not been brought on, he continued to stretch and pace along the tidy lush fringe until, as one fan had already pointed out to him, he was more tired than he had been at the end of the two matches he'd played.

And then, one morning later that week during a chest-control routine, there he was – leaving the outbuilding as though that was where he had been this whole time. Tom tried not to look. He concentrated on the drills, sprinting, jumping, heading, attempting to distract himself from the hollow racing sensation in his stomach that grew each time there was an interval of quiet from the steady hum of the mower. At the end of the session he came in with the others. He showered, turning the knob to its coldest until he was nearly unable to breathe.

The next day he continued to look away. Only during the runs, when they jogged in a long column, would he allow himself to watch him. And it was at these times that he would see him looking, as if at the whole squad, from where he sat on the mower or rolled crisp, shocking-white lines onto the grass.

The rest of the squad had showered and changed, but Tom stayed sitting in his towel on the splintered bench until they had all left. Even though he had stopped training alone nobody waited for him any more or asked if he was coming to the canteen or the pub. He sat there for some time before he put his clothes on, then left the room, stepped into the cold prefab corridor, and began walking to the car park.

He got into his car, which was parked to one side where the gravel surface dipped slightly towards nettle bushes and a low dead tree, and waited.

The man was one of the last to leave. The assistant manager, the physio, some of the players and the canteen staff had all got into their cars and driven off while Tom sat there.

He felt his blood throbbing against the headrest as he observed him in his rear-view mirror, coming up the path, calmly approaching the blue car parked on its own in the middle of the car park. He got in and – Tom could just make out his movements through the windscreen – adjusted his radio or something on the dashboard for a moment before starting the engine and slowly pulling away.

The team won another match, away, resoundingly. Tom did not play. His dad called him afterwards and said that he wanted to come down and see him, or for Tom to come and spend a few days at home. Tom lied and told him that neither would be possible, because the manager was making them do extra, and longer, training sessions. His dad told him again to be patient and keep his sleeves rolled up, that his chance would come, eventually.

One week on from the reappearance of the groundsman Tom was sitting in the canteen, surrounded by the smell of deodorant and soft exhausted food, at the long central table around which the squad were athletically devouring jacket potatoes, baked beans, chips, chilli con carnes. He was on the bench at one end of the table, facing away from the entrance, and so did not at first see the groundsman coming in. Only when he had come past and stood at the hot grubby glass of the display cabinet did Tom spot him. He was waiting for the server to come back through from the kitchen. Tom watched the back of his head anxiously as he looked down at the cracked empty dishes and the remaining jacket potatoes. Only when he took his plate of potato and beans and walked, without looking over, to an empty table on the other side of the room did Tom notice Balbriggan, sat opposite him, following the man's movement. Tom went still with fear when he saw the small smile on Balbriggan's face as he nudged Foley on the arm, nodding in the direction of the groundsman.

Foley looked around, baffled, not sure what he was supposed to be seeing.

'You know what he is, that guy?' Balbriggan was staring across the room, his small stupid eyes proud, gleeful.

'Who?'

'Him – the new groundsman.'

Tom looked over now, too, to where the man sat by a window eating slowly and alone, his bright immaculate pitches stretching away through the window beyond him.

Foley frowned briefly, confused, as Balbriggan whispered into his ear, before turning back to what was left of his chilli con carne.

Tom sat in his car with the radio on low as the other vehicles departed one by one until only a few remained.

Balbriggan had continued talking to Foley for some time after they turned their attention away from the groundsman. He complained about the grass, that it was too long, that it should be a fucking rugby pitch. Tom had sat there listening to them as anger, and pity, raged inside him, making him want to stand up and damage something, to damage Balbriggan, to pick up his plate and smash it on the top of Balbriggan's dense tanned head. He stayed there with his meal half finished until those two and a few of the other players had left the canteen. The man must have been aware of him. He wondered if he was aware too of what the players said about him. Tom looked across only once. He was still eating, his head bent towards his food; the wide, open face difficult to read. Tom had felt again that same faint sadness as when he'd watched him press in paint-pot lids on the table in front of the old club scarf. He stood up, walked over to put his tray onto the stacking tower by the door and left.

The manager was leaning on his sunroof, talking into his phone.

Tom could not fully hear what he was saying but he made out 'board' and 'spastic' before the manager flipped the phone shut and got into his car to leave. When the sound of the engine had died down the lane and the car park was again in silence, Tom got out. Quickly, looking around him, he walked towards the blue car. He stopped for a few seconds in front of it, looking through the windscreen at the few scattered CDs and payslip envelope on the mucky passenger seat, before stepping forward and pulling out one of the windscreen wipers. He checked over his shoulder, then placed a piece of paper onto the glass and let the wiper retract to pin it in place. Only one word had been written on it, in large letters, slightly crumpled now under the pressure of the wiper. Faggot. Tom stared at it for a moment, then turned, walked unsteadily back to his car, started the engine and drove away.

LAURA DEL-RIVO

J KRISSMAN IN THE PARK

HIS OUTFIT WAS not absurd on an old man in midwinter: knitted ski cap, secondhand coat of good quality and bright white trainers. Privately, to conserve warmth, he was bandaged in a winding sheet of thermal underwear and tubular medical crepe. The frail knees were anointed with menthol.

J Krissman, the name with which he signed his unpublishable writings, experienced his body as an immediate area of seepage and discomfort. His organs, however, persisted with their functions, such as the filtering of his urine; the skin shed its comet dust of dead cells. Also the skeleton, the specific diagram in bone laced with dainty capillaries, advanced him through the black, green and copper-tinted urban park.

The winter light made the trees distinct. Pollarded branches ended in bristling knuckles. High in the tallest tree, a slovenly heap of dead vegetation was unmoved by the wind. Krissman considered whether it was possible to quantify in terms of physics the stillness of the squirrels' dray which seemed in a different dimension from the tonnage of surging air. He remembered that the purpose of his walk was to purify a letter.

His mouth contained the protein odour of the digestion of dead plants and animals, and words.

'I read your article in the *New Scientist* on Multiverse Theory describing two hypothetical Universes, one predicated on a cold Big Bang and the other lacking the Weak Nuclear Force. I need to ask, is there a law which states that if the Universe can exist, it must exist?'

As he spoke, he experienced agitation and wonder, as if winged archangels had sprung up at his shoulders.

'That is, is the hypothetically possible the same as the necessary?'

Due to the opaque property of matter to the handicapped human eye, the remaining body of Krissman showed no immodesty of skull or bone, no unseemly lolling of lights and liver. He leaked only mild warmth, which activated the volatile film of menthol. However, he was in a rage and pain because in old age his mind as well as his body was becoming uninhabitable. The cause of such turmoil was that he hated humanity, its mass and mediocrity. The hatred had set up camp in his mind and its angry and unpleasant manoeuvres without cessation gave him no rest. He chose the park for his daily walk to avoid as much as possible the pinkish mass of foolish faces.

Among J Krissman's rejected writings, THE ANIMAL NOT SOLIPSIST BUT CREATIVE proposed that meaningful existence depended on its being verified and recorded by a life form conscious of being conscious. The author argued that knowledge is secondary creation; thus the dinosaurs were retrospectively brought into full existence. Their terrifying reptilian roar would have been silent without ears. However, by this argument, his own unpublished work did not exist.

It seemed clear to him that, for serious purpose, humanity was overproduced. Its billions were unnecessary; it was devalued by quantity. He wished it no harm but refused the imperative to love the massed pinkness, which was unloveable. In crowds, the unlovable became the hated.

Sometimes he felt as if wolves were eating his mind, but he did not know whether the wolves were other people or generated by himself.

For these reasons, it was necessary for his safety to bandage also his mind, which was more obscene than the stained and discoloured rags of flesh.

Me Oh Lord You have made to hate. I am even vain of my hatred, believing I am Your chosen hater. By anomaly I am an atheist and supporter of most liberal causes.

The pollarded branches clubbed the sky. The squirrels' dray was undisturbed.

The most dangerous was that the hatred was spreading from his mind to his soul and narrowing his ability to experience wonder.

A family group occupied a bench. Surrounding them like a gilded bubble was the superpower of the commonplace. Of the two young women, one held a pram containing a baby while a boy of about four clung to the pram handle. A youth, possibly the women's brother, who accompanied them, shared their sacramental Tesco biscuits.

This family represented the social class, which Krissman most feared and hated, that proliferated in council estates.

The cold made him nauseous. His hands were plagued by black tokens; he pressed one subcutaneously bleeding hand over his liver which seemed swollen in its caul. The containment of such hatred was feverishly painful to Krissman. Being rational by type, he tried to analyse his hatred; that is, he tried to hold down and analyse the thing that was painful while the pain was most severe. It was revealed to him that he suffered from frustration of the will: that he willed these people not to exist but they did exist.

He was persecuted by their existence.

The wind dragged shapes through the grass around their bench; their wrappings of biscuits and crisps were also blown.

He dared not speak his thoughts aloud: 'You are unnecessary and therefore vile. Your love is complacent.'

The virtue of the young women was that they were ordinary and loving. The power of the ordinary overwhelmed that of the wretched Krissman. The quite pretty sisters hardly noticed him; then fluently dissed him:

'Ohmygod, how spazz was that?'

Nothing had happened except that an old man had passed a family in a park. The space between buildings was not even a park; only a public gardens with trees, squirrels and benches. At the gate, Krissman turned his mind to the article which had described the other two viable universes. There would be few or no visible stars. He was too uneducated in physics and maths to expand his mind but the effort of trying to do so for several seconds expanded his soul.

ALEX PRESTON

THE SWIMMER IN THE DESERT

HE SPITS OVER the side of the tower and pats the handle of the revolver in his belt. The first silver line of dawn traces the outline of the mountains and he realises he can hear water. He has heard it before in the morning but never this clearly.

Even the night air feels as if it has been breathed a million times, as if some desert djinn is panting stale air straight into his lungs.

The snows are melting in the high Kush, sending emissary streams needling down the slopes, feeding the wadis of the plateau, the poppy fields that glow red in the foothills. As the air around lightens, he can make out the stream in the distance.

He'd passed the dry bed a few days before, with the Multiple on foot patrol – eight hours with guns, ammo and water, climbing into the nearest hills, always walking with one foot tapping the ground ahead like a blind man's cane. They'd found an IED on the main Lashkar Gah road. A basic device buried under a mound of blue-grey aggregate. Later, he'd stood for a while in the centre of a poppy field, the heads of the flowers nodding in a warm breeze. He picked one and tore the petals off. On the way back they'd crossed the riverbed which now babbles with dark water.

He leans out over the side of the watchtower. The sun begins to rise, and not with the pink diffidence of the sun at home, but already white and cruel as it explodes over the peaks of the Kush. The coming of the light changes the sound of the water. His throat is dry and he reaches down to his belt for his flask to find it missing.

He doesn't know who has been taking his things. It has become part of a more general deprivation he barely notices. He came here because he thought it would make something of him; in fact it is unmaking him. The road leading up to the gate of the compound is lined with Hesco barriers. They look fragile, almost transparent. He imagines them as Chinese lanterns, imagines lighting them and seeing them float up into the pale sky. He looks at his watch: an hour to go.

He lifts his binoculars and follows the course of the stream. A mile to the east it passes under the lip of a rocky levee and fans out into a pool. It looks cool there in the shadows by the rocks. Silver flowers open and close on the sandstone lip that juts above the water as the sun catches the stream. He hasn't swum since he's been here.

He remembers swimming with Marie. They rushed past Dawsholme Park, over the canal, and then they were in the countryside. They pushed their bikes up the steepest part of the hill and then stood on the crest looking down. Two lochs – Jaw and Cochno – separated by a narrow isthmus. After their swim, when they dried off on the banks of the loch, she looked around with quick, narrow eyes and unfastened her bikini top, letting the sun and his gaze fall upon her as she stretched out on the grass. When he kissed her it felt like they were swimming again, nervelessly, over deep water.

It is time for his relief. The sun is higher now, near-unlookable. He hears the reveille – a short, brutal blast over loudspeakers, and the clatter of breakfast being prepared in the mess. Someone is singing in the shower block.

His relief is late. The sun detonates above him, raging into the space behind his eyes. He's aware of every patch of exposed skin. He tries to think of Marie in the loch, but it is too distant and cool a picture. He looks over towards the pool of water and sees it is still in shadows. He feels an urgent need to swim. He imagines standing on the lip of the levee and hurling himself into the water.

An hour passes. He is sitting in the narrow band of shade on the floor of the watchtower, not even pretending to keep watch.

Every so often he rises and scans the maze of tunnels for sign of his relief. He knows that they want him to leave his post. That some shameful plan was hatched over beers in the mess last night, the snaking path of its plot ending in his humiliation. He feels himself pitching as if on a boat. He rises again, but this time, binoculars to his eyes, he looks at the pool.

More than anything now, he wants to feel water on his body. He would choose swimming water over drinking water. He knows about the water gardens in this part of the world, the wide avenues of whispering trees and fountains. There is a religion of water here. He can understand that. He can see that God is dancing in the water under the levee.

He climbs down from the watchtower. His joints creak, his binoculars slap against his neck, his sweat spirals to the ground beneath the ladder. He pauses at the compound gates. With a sudden instinct, in the free space where solid thought forms, he reaches out and opens the door that is set into the right-hand gate. Still walking, he steps through and out into the world.

He sets off briskly across the fulvous earth. His feet are scorched by the heat, torn by the sharp spines of scrub, cut on rocks. He begins to run. He takes off his jacket and lets it drop to the ground behind him, peels off the white T-shirt to reveal a bone-thin body. He doesn't even think about IEDs. He draws in a deep breath of air and lets it out with a low, delighted whoop. In the mountains above he catches a momentary flash of sun on glass, ignores it, and presses on. He is sprinting now, leaping rocks and brush.

When he comes to the levee he looks back to the compound and sees the watchtower is still empty. He undoes his belt, pulls down his trousers, his boxer shorts, is suddenly pleased by the burn of the sun on his body. He edges to the lip of the levee and stands there, angeline on the rim of a cloud. There is a crack, and it is the sound of a body plunging into water, the sound of thunder, the sound of a rifle shot in hill country.

He plunges downwards into this water that remembers when it was snow. Water that wound between grazing goats, through poppy fields, beside the small house where two of the young men live who now stand above the stream, looking in.

The water carries in it iron, zinc, silica, traces of goat and human faeces, the spit of a grandmother from Chitral, opium and poppy stems, the petals of flowers from a wedding at Kachil, potassium, magnesium, gunpowder, human and dog urine, the sweat of a man who bathed that morning at dawn in Tang e-Gharu. Despite the weight of all this, the water bounds along the stream bed, dancing and tear-clear. The young men shoot their guns into the pool for effect and then scamper back to the truck at the foot of the levee.

Already the force of the current has carried his body onwards, over jagged shallows where it roils white, into another, deeper pool, where swimming creatures are congregating, insect larvae thrusting themselves from the bed into green depths. His foot snags on a root and he is caught, trembling, in the stream, his eyes wide and bright under the water. A plume of blood escapes like the ghost of a watersnake from the hole in his head, is caught by the current, and carried away.

ADAM LIVELY

VOYAGE

He glanced across the table. Stalin had cracked a joke. He was the only one who ever joked. None of them laughed – not even Stalin. But Stalin did crack jokes. And he had an unpleasant smile, almost hidden by his bushy moustache. The others didn't even smile.

They talked politics. They understood little of what each other said – just the odd word like 'fascism' and 'communism'. It didn't matter. To begin with, he seemed to remember, they had talked across each other. Then the realisation must have come that they had all the time in the world. Stalin could talk through the entire main course and it wouldn't matter because the next night it would be someone else's turn.

Or that was what he thought had happened. He looked down at his plate. *Coq au vin* – undercooked chicken and some slivers of onion in a watery brown gravy. It was hard to remember anything. He couldn't remember the waiter bringing the dish. The waiters were hazy – the only faces that were clear were those across the table. All he knew was that the food was disgusting. It made him think of a railway hotel in some small town in the Bavarian highlands – the kind of place where he'd spent solitary nights early in his career after giving a speech to the local party, the kind of place where the waitresses wheeling the sweet trolleys were middle-aged and built like barrels.

The sudden glimpse of a memory, of sanity, was unsettling. He looked up. Stalin had turned serious. He was winding up his speech on a serious note. When he had finished and wiped his moustache with his napkin, Franco immediately started up, adopting the same tone – quiet, sententious. He hated the way the Spaniard toadied to Stalin – always speaking after him, aping him as though he were some clerk clarifying a few minor points. Franco looked like a bank manager. He looked like one of the local party officials who would introduce him in those depressing Bavarian towns sunk between the hills. He had hated them. And now he hated Franco.

After dinner they dispersed. He would take a turn on deck. The first moment when he stepped through the door was good, when for a few seconds the air would be fresh on his face and the sound of the sea would be booming. But then the door would slam shut behind him, the night enfold him. He walked a few paces along the deck and looked out over the rails. Always the same view – the mist and the night. Far below, the foam of the bow wave was luminescent on the inky water. The ship was moving fast. It was always moving fast. He looked back down along the long length of it. Franco had said that it had used to sail the Buenos Aires–Lisbon route – but then what did he know? And how had he understood him even if he had said that? He couldn't remember. Nothing made sense.

Far in the distance, down the length of the ship, he could see lights in some of the portholes. Who occupied those cabins? The only other person he ever saw on deck was Stalin. He would be walking in the distance, or he would suddenly come upon him, huddled up in a deckchair with a coat wrapped around him, staring out at the mist. They never spoke. He never saw Mussolini or Franco out on deck. He had no idea what they did after dinner.

He would only stay out on deck for ten minutes or so before making his way back to bed. Every night as he approached his cabin door, down the familiar narrow corridor, he would feel the same niggle of anxiety. There was something wrong with the overhead light in his cabin. When he flicked the switch beside the door it never worked. There were only five paces between the door and the safety of the bedside lamp, but those five paces meant that for a few seconds after the door had swung shut he was in darkness, stepping blindly into darkness, fumbling in darkness for the switch to the bedside lamp. He never liked that darkness. By the time his finger closed around the switch (its feel was familiar to him, he had been feeling it for ever) his body was covered by a light sheen of sweat.

In the pool of yellow light, he undressed and put on his pyjamas.

The next thing he ever remembered was going down the corridor to dinner again. Mussolini was having his dessert – Stalin and Franco were watching him intently as he stuffed his face with the cream from a gateau. Mussolini was the only one who seemed to enjoy the food. There were only three desserts on the menu and four main courses. All of it was revolting. The cream on the gateau wasn't even real – it was the powdered variety. But Mussolini was like an eating-machine. Every night he ate as though this night were his last and he might never eat again. The others, even Stalin, only ever picked at their food.

The Italian was in the middle of an anecdote. After he had swallowed several large spoonfuls of cream he put down his spoon and continued where he had left off. A dribble of cream remained on his chin. He extended one hand with its palm up and inclined his head in that direction, saying something in a wheedling, whiny voice. Then he extended the other hand and did the same thing in the other direction. It seemed to be an anecdote about conflicting counsel from his advisors. After he had done these voices, back and forth, for a minute or so, he pulled himself straight upward and slammed a fist down on the table. The cutlery bounced. This was him, Mussolini, now. He was being decisive.

When Mussolini stopped speaking there was a long silence.

He stared down at the *coq au vin*. Then Franco started murmuring. He ran a finger round his collar. It was too tight. It was always too tight. He wore a woollen civilian suit that was too thick for the stuffy atmosphere in the ballroom of the ship. They always wore the same clothes – Stalin wore a blue-grey party tunic, Mussolini and Franco military uniform, while he was in a woollen suit that was too hot and a civilian shirt and tie that was done up too tight at the neck. He looked across the table at Franco. How was it that Franco wore a military uniform with a loose collar, while he wore a civilian suit that was too hot with a shirt and tie that were too tight at the neck?

It was a relief to get out on deck. But he only stayed there ten minutes, because it wasn't till he was back in his cabin that he could take off that shirt and tie. Before that there was the light switch to find in the darkness. And it seemed only moments after he had put on his pyjamas in the pool of yellow light from the bedside lamp that he was once more walking down the corridor towards the ship's ballroom, pulling with his finger at the stiff collar that pressed into his neck.

The table at which they sat was on a curved terrace above the dance floor of the ballroom. There were other tables on the terrace, but none of them were ever occupied. The dance floor was deserted.

Sometimes, though, the dance floor would be filled by a spectral presence. Tables would appear, and there would be men at the tables. There was talking, sometimes even laughter. Their presence was an indefinite blur, but from time to time out of the blur faces would appear. Brown faces. Black faces. For a moment they loomed out of the obscurity, bearing on their lips an introduction, an obsequy. They bore names on their thick lips – Amin, Mobutu, Pol Pot, Saddam. He shivered with an old disgust at these alien faces. The glimpse of a memory, of sanity, was unsettling.

Occasionally these blurred, spectral presences would occupy the lower tables of the ballroom. He was unsure how much his companions at the top table were aware of their presence. And then they were gone, and he would be staring down at his cold *coq au vin*, waiting for the meal to finish. He went out on deck again and walked to the front of the ship. The speed of the vessel was palpable. He looked out from the prow into the darkness. A million tiny droplets of water crashed into his face. He had a vivid sense of the speed of the massive ship as it forged ahead into the darkness, of the mist as a solid substance through which it moved swiftly, unendingly.

The thought came to him that while he listened night after night to the others at the dinner table, he never said a word himself. Then another thought came to him: that it was the same for them too. They all four barely experienced the same reality.

He turned, thinking of the darkness and the light switch. He looked down the corridor. He felt the sweat in the darkness and his finger closed around the light switch. He watched the pyjamas in the pool of yellow light. His finger tugged at his collar and he listened to the confusing talk across the table. Around him was the deserted deck of the vast liner. Beneath him was the ceaseless thrust of the engine.

CHARLES LAMBERT

CURTAINS

WHEN HELEN GETS back from the hospital the house is empty. She leaves her weekend bag by the door and wanders from room to room, the kitchen, the hall, the living room, and then upstairs, pausing for breath on the halfway landing, her hands folded over her stomach. She rests her hand on the door to David's study, glances into their bedroom but doesn't enter, then stands at the threshold of the smaller room she had begun to think of as *his* bedroom or *her* bedroom, she wasn't sure, not then, until a twinge of pain across her abdomen sends her scuttling to the bathroom. David knew I'd be home this morning, she thinks, blouse pulled up, leaning her bare skin against the basin. He could have closed the shop for half an hour or asked one of the Saturday girls to come in. She waits for the pain to pass, then splashes her face with cold water.

She is sitting in the kitchen holding an empty mug when the key turns in the lock and David is home. He puts down a roll of material before hurrying across the hall, his coat half-off, to take her hand and help her up from the chair.

'You told me you wouldn't be back until this afternoon,' he says. He sounds apologetic. She can't remember what she told him, except that they would bring her home. There was no need for him to worry, it's probably her fault. He drops his coat on the floor, holds both her hands and looks into her eyes until she glances down. She wants to pull herself free and pick up the coat.

'There was no point their keeping me in any longer. All I need is rest, apparently.' She pauses, tries to smile. 'And lots of TLC.'

David lets go her hands. 'I'll make you a cup of tea.'

She shakes her head; he hasn't understood. 'No. Not tea. Make me some real coffee, will you? With the thing.' She makes a plunging gesture. 'The coffee in that place was dreadful.'

'You are feeling all right, aren't you?' He has a right to sound anxious, she thinks.

'I feel fine, David,' she says. 'Apart from, you know.'

He hugs her, finally. She rests her chin on his shoulder and stares at the material by the door. Some remnant from the shop, she imagines, some end of roll he'll expect me to do something with. To keep me busy until I'm back to normal.

'It's for the best.' He lets her go, moving her away from him as though she has no will of her own, each competent hand squeezing a shoulder, both affectionate and dismissive. She stands in the kitchen. His best, her best? Their best? David says there's no difference. For better or for worse. In sickness and in health. When the pain comes she presses her legs together to relieve it. A trickle of something warm, which must be blood, runs down her inside thigh. She watches him search for the thing she can never remember the name of, to make her coffee.

Two weeks later he walks into the kitchen with a cardboard box. It is late afternoon. She has been washing spinach; the leaves, with their thread of red, are coarse and gleaming in the colander. It makes her feel sick just to look at them.

'I've been finishing the curtains for the living room.' He moves his head rapidly to one side as if he is trying to dislodge something from his ear. The box will contain some bone he's had sent to him for his study, some fossilised knuckle from Uzbekistan he's ordered on the net. He doesn't have time to think about curtains.

'Look what I've brought you.'

She wipes her hands. He'll expect something from me, excitement, she thinks, some sign of pleasure. She's relieved, she's not sure why.

'What?' she says. She waits for him to kiss her; he always does since she came back from the hospital, a kiss on her cheek, sometimes the back of his fingers, his knuckles, against her skin. Once he took her face in his hands and stared into her eyes until she blushed, she felt like a suspect with a terrible secret. But today he holds out the cardboard box. It is large and has no writing on it, as though it has no business being.

'What is it?' She doesn't trust him, it strikes her. She hasn't the slightest idea what he wants. She has no secrets.

'Look inside,' he says. A noise from the box, a rustling or grating, startles her; she steps back.

He smiles. 'Don't be afraid. Open it.' He puts the box down on the table she has just cleaned and lifts a flap, as if to show her how boxes open. Lifting another, she peers inside to see something pale and soft rise towards her. She jumps back.

Impatient, David lifts out a blonde plump wriggling thing no bigger than his two cupped hands.

'It's a Labrador,' he says. 'A golden Labrador.'

Not knowing what to do, she takes the puppy and presses it to her, in the hollow just below her chin. It wriggles until it can lick her hand, its tongue warm, oddly dry. She lifts its face to her face; it paws her cheek, and she drops her head slightly as if for a kiss, then tilts the body to see what sex it is. Male. A twist of blond hair like a paintbrush.

'Their eyesight isn't up to much at this age,' David says. 'It's probably wondering what you are. All it can see is a great big lump.'

'How old is he?' She stresses the *he* a little.

'Six weeks.'

'Isn't that too young to be taken away from the mother?'

David's face goes hard and closed, the way it does when she tries to talk to him about his fossils, about what he sees in them. Soon after they met he told her, *You'll think it's wrong, I know, but I can't bear criticism of any kind*. And she said: But why should I want to criticise? You're perfect. She remembers this often and the one thing she can never remember is what she meant when she said *You're perfect*.

'Well? Do you want it or not?'

She looks into the puppy's eyes, moving him closer until the outline blurs, and they don't change at all, they are turned towards hers, both deep and flat. It's true, she thinks, he really can't see me. He can't see what a great big lump I really am.

'Of course I do,' she says.

Helen has spent the last fortnight making curtains from the roll of Indian silk David brought home from the shop. It was his father's shop before him, but David's never really settled. He told her before they were married he'd dreamed of becoming a palaeontologist, not of working behind a counter, that no son of his would be trapped the way he's been, not without seeing the world. That was when she agreed that children weren't needed to make a marriage work. The silk was damaged in transit, he said, but *Look how beautiful it is*, and he rolled it out in front of her across the living room floor, the way he does with the customers along the counter. He's right, of course, it is beautiful, a rippling mustard yellow shot with threads of red and royal blue. It should have been saris, he says, but the colours have muddied along one border, it must have been left to stand in filthy water at some point. So now she is making curtains for all the windows, cutting and sewing and lining them with beige cotton, also from the shop. All the windows except for the one in the small bedroom. She goes in there every day and lies down on the bed that should have been a cot, with a pillow on her stomach, staring at the bare glass. She never imagined he'd take her at her word.

David takes her out to the hall and shows her the basket he has brought for the puppy. He has been planning this, Helen thinks, this surprise. She wonders if everything in her life will be a surprise from now on, with this same flatness. The basket is made of wicker and lined with tartan, with a tartan cushion. She puts the puppy down and he sniffs the cushion, lifts its corner with his claws. He falls onto his side and lets out a startled yelp. His belly is hairless, white, with pale brown marks like coffee stains.

'We'll have to come up with a name for it,' says David, standing back, arms crossed in judgement.

'Him,' she says. 'It's a him.'

'A name for him.'

She thinks for a moment.

'Chester,' she says.

Chester amuses and irritates Helen in equal measure. She sits at her sewing machine, working at the curtains, her right foot rocking the treadle, and the puppy darts and stumbles around her, only to totter and sit down abruptly on his haunches. He's like a toy, she thinks, all fur and softness, his large brown eyes too liquid to be real. It is hard to believe he has a heart and brain; hard to believe he can feel and think. She almost wants to hurt him, sometimes, to make sure. She picks him up and he snuffles at her neck. When she tickles him he bites her finger with needle-sharp teeth until she squeals with pain and pulls away. Now and again, she forgets he's there. Her foot works the treadle more slowly and finally stops and she only realises she is crying when she feels Chester's cold damp nose against her ankle, the puppy's claws on her bare calf as he tries to scramble up to her lap, to drag his way up to her lap and nestle there. She doesn't know whether to laugh or cry, but she's already crying, so she laughs and scoops him up. She walks around with him cradled in her arms, belly up, his penis plump with its honey brush. Then, out of the blue, a wave of sadness overwhelms her and she puts him down, almost throws him to the floor.

She doesn't take him upstairs, into the small bedroom. Later, coming down, distracted by his yapping, she sees that he has peed on the hall carpet. He whines and capers around her feet, beside himself with excitement, while she scrubs at the stain with a damp cloth. I could do anything to you, she thinks, picking him up, holding him out as far as she can reach, watching him wriggle in her hands in his attempt to lick them. You're as helpless as a child.

She doesn't tell David about the pee. When he takes off his coat and says 'Have you two had a good day?' she smiles and nods. 'I've finished the curtains for the living room,' she says. 'I'll need your help to put them up.'

She follows him through the door, his narrow shoulders before her. 'There's enough left over for cushions. I thought I might make sausage ones, for the sofa.' But David is examining her hems, his glasses on, lips pursed. 'Lovely work,' he says after a moment, during which Helen feels as though she has turned on the TV to see familiar people whose names escape her, in a room she knows but can't recognise. She watches, fascinated but anxious. I've lost the plot, it occurs to her, and she wants to giggle because she has never understood this expression before today. David has taken off his jacket and is waiting by the window, one foot on a low stool, his shoes taken off and placed beside the stool. He is wearing those fine sheer cotton socks that look like stockings, Helen can't bear them. David must have them dry-cleaned, or wash them himself, in secret. If they turned up in the laundry basket she'd lose them, one by one, she'd tear them open with her hands. He'd last two seconds digging for fossils, she thinks. 'You've done a lovely job,' David says. They both step back to see how beautifully the curtains hang.

That night, when she thinks he's asleep and she is staring at the ceiling waiting for light, he turns his whole body until it is pressed against her side, his minty breath in her face, his soft sly hand slipping down between her legs. 'I don't suppose,' he whispers. 'Oh no, David,' she says. 'Not yet.' 'A little loving,' he says, his throat dry. 'I'm sorry,' she says, but she isn't. She's appalled and disgusted. I wish I was dead, she thinks, I'll never sleep again. But she must have gone to sleep, because she wakes in shock with the image of her dead baby floating in front of her eyes, the small plump hands reaching out towards her through an impenetrable wall of water.

David brings her coffee, but it makes no difference. Fifteen minutes later, he's back with Chester yapping and wriggling in his arms. He's holding the puppy at arm's length from his cashmere sweater. She can't resist reaching out, as much for David's sake as for Chester.

'Cushions today?'

'What?'

'You'll be starting on the cushions?'

'I expect so.'

'We could go out for a bite together this evening,' he says, cautious. 'It would save you cooking. There's a new place near the Library the girls were talking about. Turkish, I think they said. It would do us both good to get out.'

'We can't leave Chester all alone,' she says.

'Well, think about it,' he calls from the stairs. 'I'll talk to you later.'

When they get back from the restaurant, David slightly drunk, Helen more tired than she can ever remember, as though her strength has been ripped from inside her, like stuffing, the living room floor is covered with scraps of yellow silk, chewed into rags. David stumbles to the curtains, tripping over the stool, saying 'I don't believe it', but Helen catches his arm before he can fall. 'It's only the cushion material.'

In the hall, she calls, 'Chester,' her voice low and soft, coaxing. She makes her kissing noise until he sidles over. He knows he's done something wrong, whatever the books say about guilt. David is behind her, but she doesn't turn round until she has scooped the puppy up and is holding him close.

'He needs to be punished,' David says. He's slurring in a way that revolts her. In the restaurant, he'd had a smear of hummus on his chin, like a baby. She'd left it there, not saying anything, hoping he wouldn't wipe it off before the waitress he'd been flirting with had seen him. Of course, he'd deny it. He'd say she was imagining things.

That was the first time David talked about punishing Chester. The second time, they come back from the weekly shop to find one of his precious cotton socks chewed into a sodden hank. Helen doesn't recognise it immediately; she thinks it's something dead. David yelps, as though a sticking plaster has been ripped from his skin. She puts the bags down on the kitchen table. 'It's only a sock,' she says, taking out packets of rice, pasta, a box of eggs, searching for the treats she's bought for Chester, three months old now and stronger than she is.

'You spoil that dog. He needs a sound thrashing.'

And you're going to give him one, I suppose, she says, too low for him to hear. She wonders what kind of father he'd have made. Some days it's as if she's the one who deprived *him* of their child, not the other way round, and she feels a sort of exultation she can't explain, that frightens her, as though she were capable of anything. *You* need a sound thrashing, she wants to say. *You* need to be punished. But she doesn't move when David grabs Chester's collar and drags him across to the kitchen door. She watches him fumble one-handed with the lock while the dog resists, the blond fur on his forehead wrinkling into a frown, his front paws stretched out for purchase. She lets him lock Chester out until the dog's whimpering gets on his nerves, not *her* nerves, and David allows him back into the house.

She's lying on the bed in the little room, where the cot would have been, thinking about post-natal depression, wondering if what those women feel is what she's feeling, or if you need to have had the child, and how different that might have been, and if what she feels is depression or something else, something nameless, something she doesn't care, or dare, to name. Chester's outside the door, crying, but she's closed herself off to that. You're David's dog, she says, out loud, to no one. He asked her yesterday evening, while they were watching television, why she'd called him Chester. She didn't answer, she pretended she hadn't heard. He'll stop in the end, he always does, and then she'll get up and go downstairs.

But she doesn't go downstairs, not immediately. She opens the door to David's study and stands at the threshold, staring at the walls with all their shelves of books and index boxes and glass-fronted displays of fossils, arranged in some way she isn't expected to grasp, and so has never tried. Lowering her eyes, she looks at the table in the centre of the room. It's covered with grey-white bones laid out in the form of an animal, she supposes, the fragile net of all that's left of something the size of an adult cat, or small dog. For one shocked moment she imagines he's building a human child.

David's decided to take control of Chester. He gets home from the shop and clips the lead onto his collar, then drags the dog out of the house and round the block. This takes just over nine minutes, nine minutes and twenty seconds to be precise; she knows because she's watched the clock. When they come back into the kitchen, Chester leaps up to lick her face, almost knocking her out of her chair, then bounds across to David, who's hanging the lead on its hook. 'That's what he needs,' he says with satisfaction. 'It would do you good as well, a little exercise.' The dog's so excited he's done a puddle by the bin. As far as he's concerned she might as well not be there, so she'll let David mop the floor clean. But he goes up the stairs. She listens to him open and close his study door, listens to him turn on the light and cross to the table, and she wonders why he doesn't take Chester with him. Dogs, after all, love bones.

The next evening, and every evening after that, David follows the same routine, arriving home from the shop and taking Chester round the block before going up to his room until it's time to eat. She no longer checks the time. While they're out she goes to his study and walks to the table and rearranges the bones, so slightly he might not even notice. She's downstairs in the kitchen by the time he comes back; it never occurs to him to ask what she's been doing.

He doesn't seem to enjoy the walk any longer. He complains to her that Chester pulls, and barks. 'I thought you were doing it for him,' she says, but David has already gone and the dog is resting his muzzle on her knee and staring up at her with his eyes that only seem to mean something, she knows that. She doesn't have any idea how long she's been sitting there, stroking his head, when David runs down the stairs.

'Have you let the dog into my room?'

'Of course not,' she says.

'Well, someone's been in there.'

She can hear he wants to accuse her, but daren't. He's been scared of her for weeks now, ever since the hospital.

'Things have been moved,' he says.

'What things?'

'You wouldn't understand,' he says and swings out of the room.

'Try me,' she calls out. To her surprise, he's back within seconds.

'If you can't keep that dog under control,' he says, his voice trembling, 'I'll have it put down.'

She was eight years old when her parents took her to Chester Zoo. They were in the mammal house when she saw a tapir lying on its side and a woman in zoo overalls hurrying across. Something damp and glossy and black was coming out of the tapir's bottom. It's doing a poo, she was about to giggle to her parents, but the poo began to move and the woman in overalls was waving across the compound for help as the tapir twisted its stubby trunk round to sniff at the thing it had made and lick the glossiness off. Later that afternoon, she'd been sick, after too much ice cream and pop. Let that be a lesson to you, her mother said.

David doesn't take the dog out again. He's taken to locking the door to his study, so her small work on the bones has been interrupted, but that's all right. She thinks about making the cushions she planned to make, but Chester has ripped up the remaining fabric. She watches television and wonders how to ask him why he made her kill her baby, how to broach the subject in a way that won't make him feel he's being picked on. But none of this is enough. One day she takes her scissors and cuts the fabric she needs from the living room curtains, a strip the height of her knee, throwing away the lining. She sets to work, with Chester beside her. By the time David's home that evening, the cushions are finished.

But she doesn't have time to show him the cushions before he's shouting and waving the curtains at her. She's cut them so roughly they might as well have been torn, she can see that now, so it's hardly surprising he blames the dog. Well, let him, she thinks. He's left the house before she can say a word. By the time he comes back, much later, she's hidden the cushions beneath the bed in the small room, where he never goes.

She's in bed when he says, 'That's it.' He's standing at the door, his toothbrush in his hand.

'That's what?'

'The next time that dog does anything, anything at all,' he says, 'I'm having it put down. I mean it this time.'

'You're mad,' she says, under her breath.

Three days after that, four months after the other thing, when he's almost certain to have forgotten what he said, she forces the lock to the study door with a screwdriver, tips up the table until all the bones of the creature – poor creature, she thinks, poor innocent creature – are scattered across the floor, then grinds them into powder beneath her heel. She's already made the appointment at the vet's. Chester doesn't want to come at first, but she's popped some treats in her pocket. She'll stay with him right up to the end; it's the least she can do. She'll get back in the car, with the useless lead and collar in her bag, and drive home. She'll be waiting in the small bedroom when David gets there. She'll know by then that what she has done is wrong and that nothing she can do will put it right.

ANNELIESE MACKINTOSH

DOCTORS

CONGRATULATIONS AND HURRAY for you!

What you have achieved is no mean feat. It makes you kind of special. Heroic, even. Not only did you get your Masters, you wee genius, but you got a Distinction. That's right; with a capital 'D'. You can put M.Litt. at the end of your name now, if you want. You can show off about this for the rest of your life.

Thank goodness you didn't go to Paris to become a mime artist, like you said you would. Christ no, that Masters was definitely the right choice.

And by golly, you learnt so damn much. What did you learn again? You learnt that writing doesn't have to be like a million fireworks all going off at once. You learnt that you shouldn't try to illustrate your own work. You learnt that you have a distinctive and original voice. You learnt that having lunch with famous authors is overrated. And you learnt that it is possible to lose a condom inside yourself during a one-night stand, only to find it two days later while doing a wee, oh horror, oh horror.

So what did you do after your Masters then, you whiz kid, you? Did you pen your great novel? Move abroad? Teach poor, sick children how to read and write? No, you did not. You took a full-time job in a card shop. At the card shop, you had to polish the front of every card in the shop, every morning.

After a week and a half, you began to miss uni. You were treated like a god at uni. You had lunch with Margaret Atwood at uni. You were never asked to polish the cards or count the novelty pencils at uni.

So on your day off you went back. Standing in the English Literature office, you told the course convenor you might like to do a PhD. When he asked why, you didn't mention Margaret Atwood or novelty pencils. You said: 'Because I want to be a Doctor, like my dad.' 'Okay,' he replied, 'that's as good a reason as any.' He handed you a thirty-page application form with seventy-two pages of guidance notes, and then you polished cards and waited.

Sometime in late August, you received a letter saying your application had been successful. You were going to do a PhD. And what's more, you were going to be paid to do it.

The people at the card shop gave you an aloe vera plant when you left.

At this point you began to realise that you had no idea what a PhD actually was. All you knew was that your dad had one, in Electronic Engineering, and his had gone so well he went to America and met Bill Gates. Oh, and you had also seen PhD students around campus and knew what they looked like. So you bought yourself a few cardigans, to fit in, and practised your lunch conversation with Bill Gates, just in case.

So here you are now, you clever thing, sitting in your flat with a load of cardigans and an empty computer screen. What are you going to do first? Well, before you can write anything on that lovely clean screen of yours, you're probably going to have to do some reading.

To the library!

Once there, take out books with the determination of a contestant on *Supermarket Sweep*. You told your funders you were going to research 'representations of visual impairment in literature', because it sounded impressive, so grab anything you can find about eyes and the lack of eyes and representations of the lack of eyes and *How to Do a PhD* and anything with a pretty cover.

Blimey, aren't books heavy? You'd never noticed before.

When you lug the books down to the front desk, hot and sweaty in your cardigan, ask the librarian: 'What's the maximum number of books I can take out in one go?' 'I don't know for a PhD,' he will say. 'But it's a lot.'

Smile and look at the queue behind you, hoping everyone heard that. I don't know for a PhD, he said. For a PhD. That's right, folks: a PhD! Ask for a plastic bag to put the books in and step outside into the rain.

At home, decide you are going to need a special shelf. Box up your self-help books and put your PhD books in their place. Sit at your desk and look at the shelf.

Make a cup of tea.

Watch *The Apprentice* on iPlayer.

Wonder what the term 'original research' means.

Go out to a nightclub with your friends and dance to the *A-Team* theme music.

Three days later, go to the special shelf, take a book, and begin to read. The book is about blind chimpanzees in central Africa. Decide to write a PhD on 'The correlation between visually impaired chimpanzees in central Africa and blind characters in the early novels of Charles Dickens'. Because it sounds impressive.

Open a new Word document and write that down. Then spend two and a half hours Googling for correlations between visually impaired chimpanzees in central Africa and blind characters in the early novels of Charles Dickens. Huh, well how about that? No luck.

~

Whew, you have just attended your sixth supervisor meeting, and thank goodness these exist.

Your supervisor has asked you to stop creating Word documents containing impressive-sounding titles, and to spend your time reading instead. 'Your angle will come,' he says mysteriously, and you can't help blushing at his use of the word come.

Decide that you are probably in love with your supervisor. Treat yourself to a new cardigan for your next meeting.

It is now half a year since you started, and your deliciously handsome supervisor has suggested you apply for a scholarship to study at the Library of Congress for a few months. In America. Five hundred and thirty-eight miles of books, he says, and you picture the two of you, running naked through the English Literature section, kissing by Milton and boning by Chaucer.

Miraculously, your application for a scholarship is successful, and you fly out to Capitol Hill. There, you live with two guys; one of whom is a furniture salesman, and the other of whom works in Congress. It is the start of summer, and every time you step out of the door you feel like you are being slapped in the face with a hot, wet flannel. Throw away those cardigans, girlfriend!

At the library, there is a special Center ('er'), where you have your own workspace, and there is a filter coffee machine, and you have to get your bags checked every day on the way in and out, and you feel Very Important Indeed.

Go for beers after work with your new academic friends. Get so drunk you lose your way home and fall asleep on the steps of the Capitol building. Get found by the police. When they ask where you live, tell them you can't remember. (It starts with a . . . no, wait . . .) Let them take your phone and call your housemate, telling him to come and collect you. As he drives you home at four in the morning, don't forget to tell him how sorry you are, at least once every five seconds. And cry as hard as you can when he informs you that you were asleep under his office window.

Spend the next day in bed, phoning your ex-boyfriend, your mother, your father, your sister, your friends. Get back with your ex-boyfriend, because a long-distance relationship is probably just what you need.

What you also need is routine: so find one. Arrive at the library for half nine. Leave at four. Read voraciously. Develop an interest in the representation of blind women in nineteenth-century literature. Come up with a groundbreaking theory about the description of prostitutes' eyes in the novels of Charles Dickens. Email your supervisor. Consider ending it with a kiss.

Spend evenings listening to your housemates debating politics. Understand about one sentence in ten. Go to a peacock farm owned by the furniture salesman's aunt. Lie on a sun-lounger by the pool and wonder whether getting back with your ex-boyfriend was a good idea.

Holy guacamole! You have a full draft of your PhD!

Near the end of the scholarship, your dad comes to visit. Proudly show him your place at the library. Books here, computer there, filter coffee machine over there. Take him to the Brown Bag Lunch and listen to your friend Guido play a tune on the library's Stradivarius. Does your dad look impressed? Of course he does.

Take a couple of days out from the library to go to New Orleans with your dad. Norlins, he tells you. You have to pronounce it Norlins. Listen to a jazz band on the Mississippi. Take a horse and cart ride around the French Quarter. Visit the voodoo museum. Go on a boat ride and spot eight alligators.

On your dad's last night in America, stay up late discussing your PhD. Sparkle as he tells you how proud he is. Listen carefully as he tells you how bored he gets these days, because he has no-one to talk to about clever things. Ask him if that's why he drinks so much. Get him to promise to see a doctor about his hernia when he gets back. Tell him you love him more than anyone else in the world.

When you get back to Scotland, break up with your ex-boyfriend. Shortly after that get a phone call from your dad. His hernia is sorted, he says, but now he has cancer.

See a psychiatrist.

Fly to Disneyworld with a man you have known for just two days. Then Prague with a man you have known two weeks. Consider this progress. Receive feedback from your supervisor. Edit. Edit.

See a psychologist.

Go to England and feel shocked at how ill your dad looks. Think about quitting your PhD. He tells you how proud he is of you for doing it, so don't quit, don't ever quit, just keep on going.

Back in Scotland, double your dose of antidepressants. Stop eating properly. Cry after two glasses of wine. Get herpes. Completely rewrite your entire PhD in a fortnight. (You have ditched the early nineteenth century, and are now looking exclusively at the fin de siècle. The fin de siècle is where it's at, dude.) Get a new boyfriend. Watch endless episodes of *Come Dine With Me* but stop cooking. Realise you're not really sure what the fin de siècle actually is. Return all your library books and put the self-help books back in their place.

How to Cope with Depression.

A Rough Guide to Grief.

Pulling Your Own Strings.

Phone home several times a day. Your mum tells you she wants a divorce. Your sister tells you she wants to die. Your dad tells you he has ten weeks to live.

Try cognitive behavioural therapy. Come off the antidepressants. Ask your supervisor out on a date and cry when he says no. Cry after one glass of wine. Tell your supervisor he is a total prick. (But delete the email before you hit send.) Rewrite the entire PhD again, this time only using words beginning with the letter 'c'. Come home early from a nightclub and cut yourself with a razor. Tear off a piece of the aloe vera plant and squeeze the gel onto your wound. Go back on the antidepressants. Develop a headache. Go for a brain scan.

Hurray for you, hurray for you.

Make a list of your losses over the last ten years. Map them out on A3 paper and colour-code them. Brain scan tests inconclusive. Go home for Father's Day. Decorate the patio in chalk. Draw hearts and stars and write 'I love you Graham's number' and tie balloons and streamers to the silver birch tree by the back door. Watch your dad walk across the patio with his Zimmer frame and tears in his eyes.

Just before you leave, your dad whispers something: go on lots of adventures for me.

Cry on the train all the way back to Glasgow.

Move in with your boyfriend. Phone your dad and ask his advice on plastering walls. Wish him luck for his hospital appointment tomorrow.

Build a bed.

Find a missed call from your mum the next morning.

Seven hours later, arrive at the train station. Buy a cheese and onion sandwich for your dad and head for the hospital. Wonder why your mum has stopped replying to your texts. Walk through the hospital wondering where all the people are. Find the oncology ward and reach for the door handle. A nurse stops you. 'Haven't you heard?'

In a darkened room, see your sister and your aunt and uncle. Your mum is waiting for you outside the wrong hospital entrance.

A few moments later, see your first dead body. Touch it. Talk to it. Say goodbye to it.

Drink. Cry. Edit.

It's snowing outside. Put on a cardigan. Fuck it, put on two.

Buy an extra pair of tights because your legs sting so badly in the cold, then walk tentatively towards your viva. A viva is an exam, where you get to discuss the research you've done over the last four years. To show the examiners why you are an expert, why you deserve to be a Doctor. It's the most satisfying part of your whole PhD, your dad once told you.

Two hours later, the viva is over.

Try not to slip over in the snow on the way out, and head for the nearest bar. All your friends are waiting for you. They have cards and presents, balloons and streamers. Down two glasses of champagne and open your presents.

What's wrong with a PhD composed entirely out of words beginning with the letter 'c', you ask. What's wrong with those cunting cocks – can't they cope with the concept?

Consider writing a letter to Margaret Atwood or Bill Gates. Consider writing a letter to your dad, telling him how relieved you are he's not here to see you fail.

Hurray for you.

Wonder what the hell a PhD is anyway. Then do all that you know how to do. Write.

ROBERT SHEARMAN

BEDTIME STORIES FOR YASMIN

MRS TIMOTHY NEVER wanted Yasmin to be frightened, not of anything, and she made sure that in all her picture books the lions had nice smiles and the crocodiles came with blunted teeth. Mr Timothy disagreed, and that was predictable enough; since Yasmin's birth her husband seemed to have found a way to disagree with his wife about everything. 'You can't protect her from the world,' he said. 'It's big and it's scary and it's right outside the door!' Mrs Timothy knew this was true, but it was a scary world Yasmin needn't have to confront just yet – and when it came to kindergarten, and school, and college, and all the other horrors her husband kept throwing at her, then they'd have to see, wouldn't they? – maybe some careful control would be in order. Maybe they could just do their job as loving parents and make sure Yasmin never had to mix with the wrong sort.

When Yasmin was put to bed at night Mrs Timothy would leave the light on. And she'd read her her favourite stories – about very hungry caterpillars, about beautiful princesses, about kindly folk who would never do her any harm. Mrs Timothy was not an especially good reader, and her voice inclined towards a flat monotone, so before very long Yasmin's eyes would get heavy and she'd fall asleep. And that was good, that was right, and the final image with which the story would leave her would never put her into a state of anxious suspense.

One night – only a few months ago, was it really so recent? – Mrs Timothy heard screams coming from Yasmin's bedroom, and she ran to see what was wrong. Yasmin was sitting up in bed, and she seemed to be shrinking away from the sheets, from the windows, from the wardrobe, from everything; she held her little pillow out before her as if it were a shield. 'Don't let the giants get me,' she said. It turned out that earlier that evening Mr Timothy had read her a story himself, quite against his wife's instructions, whilst Mrs Timothy was busy cooking dinner. The story had featured giants galore. Mr Timothy said, 'She seemed to be enjoying it at the time,' and Mrs Timothy opened the book and was horrified by what she saw there: men as big as houses, and stamping upon the little fairy folk, and pulling them apart like Christmas crackers, and eating them whole and raw. It took two readings back to back of Robbie the Happy Rabbit to calm Yasmin down again, and even then Mrs Timothy had had to edit out the bits where Robbie had chewed at his carrots, Yasmin didn't need to hear any more about chewing that night.

It wasn't the incident that caused the break-up, but it hadn't helped. 'You don't love me any more,' Mrs Timothy said one day, and Mr Timothy thought about it, and agreed, as if it were a revelation. 'And you don't love Yasmin either,' sobbed Mrs Timothy, 'or you wouldn't have frightened her so!' Mr Timothy said nothing to this, but he didn't deny it, so it was probably true. And that very same hour he left, he didn't even bother to pack, and Mrs Timothy was left to cry with her daughter and wonder why there was so much wickedness in the world.

Back before Mrs Timothy had become Mrs Timothy, long ago, when she'd believed everyone in the world loved her and no one would let her down, she'd had an Uncle Jack who would read her bedtime stories. Uncle Jack would come to her room after lights out and sit on the edge of her bed, and say, 'Time for a story, my pretty princess.' She didn't want to hear his stories, but the pretty princess always won her over – and she couldn't but help like Uncle Jack, he smelled so unlike her parents, and she couldn't work out why – maybe he smoked a different brand of cigarettes, or drank a different sort of beer – it was a strange smell, a *sweet* smell, as if her Uncle Jack was full of sugar – and sometimes, if she listened to one of his stories without making a single sound, he'd ruffle her hair as a treat. She knew when he began a story she should keep quiet, she mustn't scream or cry out, she mustn't even whimper – if she did, he'd simply stop the story, turn back the pages, and start all over again.

He brought the book with him. An enormous book, when he sat it down upon his lap and opened it up it was wider than he was, and she could only imagine how many stories there must be in there – hundreds, no, thousands, no, all the stories in the world. The pages were thick and heavy and as he turned them they creaked like old floorboards. He didn't turn on the lamp, he read to her by moonlight. Sometimes if the moonlight was bright enough she'd steal a look at those pages; they were dense with long words, and the words crushed tight on to the paper, and there were no pictures.

The stories frightened the girl.

One night he told a particularly terrifying story. And she tried not to, but she kept gasping out loud with fear. And each time she did, no matter how softly, Uncle Jack would hear her, and he'd stop, and back would creak all the pages, and he'd begin once more. He never seemed angry. He never seemed impatient. He read just as before, the same pace, the same wet hiss, the same emphasis on the most disturbing of words. And it was always at the exact same point that she'd gasp – five times, six times now, she could never get beyond the moment where Little Red Riding Hood admired the size of the wolf's mouth. She knew that all that was waiting for Little Red Riding Hood was death, the same horrible death that had befallen her grandmother, and she didn't even know what death was, not properly, only that it was big and black and would consume her, and once it had consumed her she'd be lost and no one would ever find her again.

Six times, seven times, eight. All through the night he read to her the same story, over and over, and each time the girl would jam her fist into her mouth, she'd hold her breath, she'd try to lie in bed stiff and hard and not move a muscle – anything, so long as the story would continue, so that the story would at last come to an end.

She fell asleep at last, for all her terror she was too tired to keep awake. And then she sat up with a start, and it was so dark, and the moonlight had gone, it was as if the moon had been switched off, and she was still terrified, and Uncle Jack was gone. His book, however, was lying on the edge of her bed.

It was her one chance to be rid of it. And yet stretching out her hand to touch it seemed such a dreadful thing. She could feel her heart beating so fast it would pop, and she wondered if that was how her parents would find her in the morning, lying dead on the bed, her fingers just brushing the warm leathery cover of a giant book; she wondered if Uncle Jack would be sad she was gone, or even care.

The book was so heavy she thought she would never lift it. Still, she did.

The house seemed different in the dead of night. The stairs made noises that sounded like warnings as she stepped on them – or maybe they weren't warnings, maybe they were threats – maybe they were calling out to the strange shadows on the wall to turn on her and eat her. The book filled her arms, as she walked ever downwards shifting its bulk from side to side it seemed she was dancing with it. She reached the back door. She unlocked it. She opened it. The blackness of the outside seemed richer and meatier than the blackness of the house, and in it poured.

She dropped the book into the bin. She slammed the lid down, in case it tried to get out again.

And then, back to her room, this time running, as fast as she could, no time to shut the back door, let alone lock it, back to her bed and under her covers before anything could eat her alive.

She had a temperature the next day, and her mother was worried, and kept her in bed. And all day long the little girl looked out of the window and hoped it would stay daytime for ever and wouldn't get dark. Because as soon as it were dark, she knew, Uncle Jack would return. And what would he say when he found out she'd thrown his book away? He wouldn't be pleased.

She couldn't sleep that night. She waited for him. But Uncle Jack didn't come.

Mrs Timothy was worried Yasmin might be disturbed by her father's disappearance, but she seemed to take it in her stride. It was her mummy who dressed her in the morning, who fed her, who read her bedtime stories. 'Sometimes things just end,' Mrs Timothy offered as explanation, and Yasmin had nodded slowly, as if she were a grown-up too, as if she could understand such things. But maybe the mistake was that Mrs Timothy had used the same phrase to explain why the next-door dog had vanished after being hit by that car; one day Yasmin frowned at her mother, she had something to ask that had been on her mind for quite a while. She said, 'Is Daddy dead?'

'Good god, no.'

'Not dead?'

'He's just away. Somewhere else. For the time being.'

But Yasmin wouldn't let it go, and eventually Mrs Timothy had been forced to call her husband. She hadn't spoken to him in a month. *Damn him*, she thought, and she felt lightheaded and girlish as she waited for him to pick up, and she was angry with herself for that, and angry with him too.

She didn't bother with a hello. 'Yasmin thinks you're dead, can you talk to Yasmin and prove you're not dead?' She handed over the phone to Yasmin before he could give a reply. Yasmin listened. Her eyes went big. She said, 'Okay.' She handed the phone back to her mother. Mrs Timothy put it straight to her ear, but her husband had already hung up. 'What did he say?' she asked.

'He's coming back soon,' said Yasmin, and smiled, and went to watch something wholesome on the television.

This is all your fault, Mrs Timothy thought, and gripped the phone tight and hard and pretended Mr Timothy could feel it, pretended she could make him hurt. *She wouldn't even know what death was without your stupid giants, if you hadn't walked out on us, if you hadn't been someone different to the man you promised to be.* And now he was causing more problems, making promises to Yasmin he wouldn't be able to keep.

She phoned him again, straight away. He didn't answer.

When the little girl grew up and became Mrs Timothy, she understood that most of the fairy tales we know today as pantomimes and Disney cartoons were much more violent and disturbing in the original. She read some of the Brothers Grimm, just to see. They were darker, it was true. But they were nothing like the gruesome stories she'd heard from Uncle Jack.

Because he'd told her of Sleeping Beauty, and how when the princess had fallen asleep for a hundred years even the maggots had thought she was dead. And some of those maggots had got sealed fast behind her eyelids, and they were hungry, so they had to feed upon the soft jellies of her eyes, and then when the eyes were gone, they burrowed their way deep into her brain. And when the prince woke her with a magic kiss the princess gazed at him with empty sockets, and her brain had turned to Swiss cheese, and she no longer knew how to speak, or how to think, or how to love. And in the summer months when the weather was hot her brain would start melting and bits of it would dribble out fat and greasy from her ears.

He'd told her of Cinderella, but that she'd had twelve wicked stepsisters, not just two, and that each night they would take turns to beat Cinderella with wire and flay off her skin. And when the prince married her, Cinderella got her revenge. And for a wedding gift she begged for the right to punish her stepsisters by whatever methods she chose. She sought counsel from all the wise men of the land, they would help her devise new tortures never before experienced by man, they would invent machines capable of prolonging each and every agony. And the stepsisters fled; and the soldiers were sent after them; and one by one they'd be caught, and tortured, and killed, and their broken corpses would be hung side by side on the castle battlements for everyone to see. But only eleven stepsisters were ever caught. One got away. And each night Cinderella would lie in bed with her Prince Charming, and she wouldn't sleep for fear that her last sister was coming to get her, that for all the guards she had posted on the door she would find a way in.

He'd told her of Snow White and the Seven Dwarfs. Snow White and the Seven Dwarfs was unspeakable.

One day, as an adult, Mrs Timothy dared to ask her parents about Uncle Jack. They had no idea who she was talking about. Her father was an only child, her mother had only sisters. Her parents didn't seem very concerned, though. This Uncle Jack, he'd probably been a family friend.

There was a scream that woke Mrs Timothy up – 'Yasmin?' she called – and only then did she realise there was a heavy storm; thunder roared above the house, lightning flashed, and rain battered hard against the windows as if it were trying to break in.

'Yasmin?' She reached her daughter's room, and the room was dark, and she tried at the light switch but it was no use. 'Sweetheart, it's just a power cut, it's all right, don't be scared.'

And as her eyes adjusted she could make out Yasmin, sitting up in bed, quite composed, pert even. 'I'm not scared,' she said.

'Did the thunder wake you? Did you see the lightning? It's all right, nothing can get at us in here.'

Yasmin didn't say anything. Mrs Timothy felt strangely embarrassed, as if she should leave. Instead she sat down on the end of her bed. 'I'll put you back to sleep,' she said. 'I'll read you a story, would you like that?'

'Yes,' said Yasmin.

'I'll read you one of your favourite stories.' She took from the shelf the tale of the very hungry caterpillar, sat back down again. Reaching for the bedside lamp she checked herself, remembered that the electricity was out. It didn't matter. She'd read the book so many times she probably knew it all by heart, and besides, there was moonlight. She opened the book, strained to make out the text. Her voice was not only monotonous, it was halting, even Mrs Timothy could hear how boring she was. Reading by moonlight was harder than she'd ever thought, she wondered how he had ever – and then she stopped herself.

'I don't want to hear about the caterpillar,' said Yasmin.

'No. Fair enough.'

'I want a different sort of story.'

'All right.'

'Let me tell *you* a story.'

'Yes. Yes. You tell me a story, sweetheart.'

Yasmin's story wasn't very good, but her voice was clearer than her mother's, and so much more confident, and she didn't hesitate over any of the words. And Mrs Timothy wanted her to stop, but she didn't think she could, she froze, and she knew that she had to keep quiet, if she made even the slightest sound Yasmin would start all over – and no, that was nonsense, of course she could make it stop, she only had to tell her to stop, this was a four-year-old girl, stop, stop, *stop*.

Yasmin stopped.

'Where did you hear that?' Mrs Timothy asked, trying to sound calm, trying to sound as if everything was normal.

'I don't know.'

'You didn't just make it up. You couldn't.' Yasmin just stared at her, her mother could almost feel her eyes boring into her. 'Who's been telling you this stuff? Who have you been talking to? Was it your father?' And she thought that, yes, maybe her little daughter was making phone calls to her husband, all behind her back, they were ganging up on her, laughing about her, Yasmin was taking sides. It was awful. It was awful. But still so much better than – 'I asked you a question, Yasmin! Was it your father?' And she was shaking her, perhaps a little too roughly.

And it was at that moment the electricity chose to come back on. And Mrs Timothy blinked in the sudden light, and saw herself grabbing on to her daughter, and she let go, ashamed. And she saw her darling little daughter's face, and it was glaring at her.

'Well,' said Mrs Timothy. 'Well.' She got up to her feet. 'Do you think you can sleep now?'

Yasmin nodded.

'Night night, my darling.' And – 'You have lovely dreams.'

Still Yasmin wouldn't say anything, but she did nestle deeper beneath the sheets.

'Night night,' Mrs Timothy said again. And made to leave the room. 'Mummy?' she heard, and turned around.

'Mummy,' Yasmin said, 'I'm sorry about the story.'

'That's all right. Never mind.'

'I'm sorry about what it's let in.'

Mrs Timothy didn't know what to say to that.

'Please,' said Yasmin, 'would you turn off the light for me?'

Her mother hesitated. Then did as she was told.

The hallway back to her bedroom seemed longer than usual, and Mrs Timothy felt cold. A flash of lightning blazed through the house for a moment, it startled her.

She reached her room, closed the door behind her.

She got into bed.

The bed was very cold, and there was a sort of dampness to the cold. It was as if the rainstorm had got in, danced lightly about her bedspread, and got out before she'd returned.

It seemed such a big bed, stupidly big, so empty without her husband, and for the first time since he'd left she wished he was there to help fill it.

She wasn't frightened by Yasmin's story. But nevertheless she decided she'd turn the light on, just for a little while. Her fingers tugged at the cord above her head. Nothing, still darkness. The power must have gone off again.

No, she wasn't frightened, that would be absurd. Indeed, she could barely remember what the story was even about now, it was already fading away like a dream – and she tried to grasp on to the memory of it, and then she made herself let it go, no, let go.

It wasn't the story that was frightening. It was what the story might have *let in*. The words popped into her head like a cold truth, and she didn't even know what that could mean – let what in? Still, it made her shiver.

She pulled up the sheets to her throat. She felt the wetness on her chin, it *was* damp. Disgusted, she threw the sheets off again. They formed a huddle on the floor by the side of the bed.

She looked around the room. She knew the room so well. She'd slept in the room for nearly four years, ever since they'd moved here, ever since she was pregnant with Yasmin. There was nothing to fear from this room. This room was her sanctuary. She had slept in this room over a thousand times, she had never been hurt here, had she? She'd never once been haunted by ghosts, or attacked by monsters, or bitten by vampires, or killed. She wished she hadn't thought of that word, 'killed'.

The shadows were bleeding out from the corners towards her. She knew why that was. The storm was doing strange things to the light, it was causing it to distort somehow, to break it into weird shapes. If she didn't like it, she could always get up and close the curtains. Get up then, close the curtains. Get up.

She didn't want to get up.

She was frightened of what the story might have let in. What had Yasmin done? She wanted to run to her bedroom, wake her, demand that she take her story back. Unsay it, make it all go away. She should get up and find her.

Oh, but she didn't want to get up, did she? Why didn't she want to get up? Think.

Because there was something under her bed. There was something under her bed. She knew it. She could sense it. If she listened closely, she could hear it whispering to her. Yes, and the moment she put her foot over the side, it would grab her, pull her under and into the darkness. Look at that body on the floor, it whispered. That could be you. – *There isn't a body on the floor, that's just the sheets I kicked off, I did that myself.* – No, it's a body on the floor.

From downstairs she heard a knock against the door.

It was just the wind, of course – but there it was again, and this time there was a rhythm to it, a tattoo of three beats, thump-thump-*thump*. And again.

It must be her husband. And she'd wanted him there only a few minutes before, but now he seemed a very real and present danger, and she wanted him gone, she wanted him off her property – he couldn't just turn up whenever he felt like, he'd made his choice, he'd made his bloody choice, and she'd go and see him and tell him just that – and she nearly got out of bed, this was something *real*, and she was just putting her foot down to the carpet when she felt it brush against her, it was too smooth and too oily, and she realised that the darkness had a texture to it now, the shadows were alive, the shadows wanted her.

She pulled her foot back to safety. The door kept knocking. *You knock away*, she thought, *I'm staying where I am.*

She closed her eyes. She tried not to think of all the darkness in her head when she did that, that the darkness she had within her might be the same darkness waiting for her without.

Thump-thump-*thump* – and then stop.

And nothing. No more of that.

And she kept her eyes closed, and stilled her breath, and listened for the slightest sound.

She heard nothing, but she *felt* it, a new weight on the end of her bed.

Her eyes snapped open, and there was nothing there – it was all right, of course there was nothing there – and she gasped with relief and thought she might even cry – and the door, her bedroom door, had she closed it? – the door was open.

She hadn't closed it. That was it. She could go and close it if she wanted to. She would, just get up and close the door. *Get up. Get up.*

What had Yasmin's story let in?

And at the doorway she saw the darkness harden, and grow denser, and turn into the shape of a person, and she thought her heart would pop – and she thought, this is how my little daughter will find me in the morning, slumped dead against the pillows, my eyes open so wide in fear, oh, Yasmin.

Yasmin?

'Is that you, Yasmin?' she made herself ask.

And the figure said, quietly, 'Yes.'

She wanted nothing to frighten her, not now, not ever. 'Were you afraid of the thunder? It's all right, darling. You sleep with me. I'll protect you. This bed's big enough for both of us.' It was *too* big, that was a certainty – and now she'd have someone to hold again, and she'd be brave, and all the ghosts and monsters could come and she'd see them all off.

The figure came in, the figure wasn't bothered by the shadows, or the darkness under the bed, or the sheet body on the floor – and the figure climbed in beside her, and Mrs Timothy had one last terror, that maybe this wasn't Yasmin after all – but it was, it was, and she could now see her clearly, this was her own little angel.

Mrs Timothy hugged her. She smelled nice and sweet. 'Don't be scared,' she told her.

'I'm not scared,' her daughter replied. She whispered it in her mother's ear.

'Good.'

Such a sweet smell, she recognised that smell. And Yasmin was slightly damp too, as if the rain had got to her. And Yasmin was right by her ear. 'Shall I finish my story?'

And Mrs Timothy pulled away from her, just for a moment, and she saw that Yasmin's eyes were too wide, and her mouth was too big for her face, and then Yasmin pulled her back, she held on to her mother's head tight so it couldn't move.

She told her story. She made her understand that there were so many ghosts, you could never tell who was a ghost and who wasn't. So very many – and some of them want to tear you apart, some of them want to drag you down to Hell – and some, if you're lucky, just want to tell you stories.

The smell wasn't of cigarettes and beer, it was of soft decay. And her touch was moist.

She told her mother her story, and her mother was good, and kept quiet during the whole thing. So she ruffled her hair before she got out of bed. And Mrs Timothy's mind still had some room to think, to wonder at how much bigger Yasmin had become, why, she looked quite the grown-up.

Yasmin stood there, and they were *both* standing there, she was holding hands with a man without a face who had just leaked out of the shadows, perhaps he'd always been there, perhaps he had been waiting all this time.

They were holding hands, they looked down at the frightened little girl in the bed like they were mummy and daddy.

It was the daddy who said, 'Sleep well, my pretty princess,' and the mummy who said, 'There'll be more stories tomorrow.' And they shrank away into the darkness of the hallway, and closed the door, and locked it.

NIKESH SHUKLA

CANUTE

THERE ARE THINGS he can't control. This comforts him. He cannot command the algorithms of nature, nor the push and pull of the tides. He knows this. He knows how deep he can go before his ears begin to throb. He knows how many lungfuls of air he can hold. But what of nature, what of the tides?

There are meetings to attend, events to accept, decline or tentative, emails to respond to, on the go, and at a desk. There are acceptable policies for workplace conduct. There are parameters and measurements and streams of code. He commands them all.

He swims to the surface and treads water. He can see his boat, 12 feet away, bobbing with whatever the waves give it. He can hear the glistening film of sun on the water. If you keep all your movements under water and stay as still as you can, you can hear the glisten and sparkle of sun rays amongst the sheer sashay of waves. He spits into his mask to clean the salt water out. He places the frame over his eyes and nose and lets go. The mask holds. He wrenches the elastic band over the back of his head and adjusts for comfort. Everything is in its right place. He closes his eyes and stops the swirl of his feet. He drops under the surface.

Poor visibility, he thinks. He can see three feet in front of him. It rained yesterday and the underwater churn has kicked up the sea bed. He must let the spearfishing forum he posts on know this. The water has engulfed him but still he can feel the itch of the speargun over his shoulder. He can't see anything to aim it at but the gun is not satisfied.

He can't see the bottom. He loves it when he can't see the bottom. He's afraid of heights. Water he understands. The first time he went skiing, with his wife Sarah, a seasoned slope fiend, he practised for an hour on the bunny slopes with the children's instructor shouting out advice from a nearby lesson. He felt like he was ready to tackle the view from the top. The visibility was poor and he couldn't see more than six feet in front of him. His heart beating, his skin burning with fright, he snow-ploughed awkwardly down the slope, scared to miss an edge in the beyond of the fog and careen to his death. He didn't enjoy himself. The next day, the air was clear and the blue sky made the white powder more ivory than he could imagine. Seeing all the way to the bottom, he found a new fear – the fear of what was to come. He didn't know what was worse – the height he could see or the height he couldn't.

Here in the water, he kicks his legs fiercely, in control of his movements, he snaps his arms back like he's tearing up a board report. He has always been a strong swimmer. He has never been afraid of water. In stasis, he is most comfortable.

A thought pops into his head as he sees a wriggle in the churn and launches himself forward, finding the culprit to be a plastic bottle: on all roads I'm alone. He saw it on a Facebook friend's wall once. He had uploaded a series of photographs of himself walking through the Mendips. The album was called 'On all roads I'm alone.'

He understands the sentiment. He works away from home three nights a week, spends a day of his weekend here in the stasis of the hunt and sees his wife for dinners. She doesn't even like fish, he smiles to himself. Breathing in this oxygen tank, he pretends he's in a spy film, searching for the microfiche hidden in the crashed pilot's cockpit.

In his office, he no longer tries to be the funny one or the lenient one. He is the boss. He is the expert. He is the rescue party.

Something catches his eye below him and he adjusts to look down at what it might be. He can't quite see it but from the movement and size he guesses it's a bass. He lets himself sink down to its level. He wonders what fish think, whether they can recognise man-made danger. You'd quickly understand what other creatures to be afraid of. Maybe not man. But wait – what's that on his shoulder? What's he pointing at me? What's that thing fizzing through the w-urgh. Does this fish know he's here to kill it and eat it, grilled with lemon and dill?

This week has been rough. A whole week away and then, on the day of the launch of his project, a server failure as they performed a company-wide software upgrade. He stayed in his hotel two extra nights. Sarah wasn't happy. It's the summer holidays and she wants to not be looking after two teenagers who are under her feet the whole time. He understands that. But it's work. It's the nature of things. He can't control it.

'I thought you said you were always in control,' Sarah said before she hung up on him. He remembers that night, that boast, when he was made redundant, decided to go freelance, she worried about their life, about the nice things going away, about her imminent skiing trip with friends while he took the kids fishing.

He's losing control, he admits to himself. It had to happen one day.

The bass has gone into the churn and he follows a trail he assumes can only be the fish's. That second of hesitation, the impasse between thought and action, has cost him his dinner.

He likes to provide. He likes this physical representation of providing. He likes that he can put food on the table, metaphorically and physically. Shame Sarah doesn't like fish.

He feels a sharp cramp in his right foot and slows down, extending and retracting the joint, trying to get the blood pumping. He's been in the water for a long time now. The wetsuit chafes against his wrinkled armpits and the creases in his arse.

Which is why that bass is his.

He swims after it, ignoring two mackerel. He feels the urgency in his toes. He cannot go home empty handed. There is nothing more important than this fish. He catches sight of the bass, which changes direction and swims down deeper. He feels an ear pop as he swerves to keep up with it.

He nearly had to give up spearfishing. His ears couldn't cope with the pressure of diving deep and coming up quickly. He was as impulsive as he was careless. He would go deep and rise up just as quickly, following the meals around him. This affected his ears, though, and he would find himself off balance. He would be sick. He would find himself using subtitles when watching television. His doctor asked him to stop. Sarah asked him to stop. He stopped. He bought himself some foraging courses, a pig and some chickens, providing mushrooms, different cuts of bacon, pork and ham, and eggs. The chickens kept the neighbours up so they were eventually eaten. The pork, bacon and ham soon dried up. The foraging carried no thrill. So he came back to the water.

Last month, he installed a new operating system for a piece of machinery that made Tupperware for takeaway restaurants. It meant half the number of staff was now needed. The company's profit margins increased by 17 per cent, significant in a recession. He had designed the software for the operating system, had worked with developers to get it right and with the company to road-test the piece of machinery. It was eventually signed off and successfully installed with no hitches. He had made that happen. He didn't work with his hands so much any more but spent his entire life designing systems for people to use their hands less.

The ballasts on his speargun rub against his side, where he bruised himself getting the boat off its trailer earlier. He winces. He considers going up to the surface. He even considers going home. Not without that bass.

A dark cloud passes over him and everything goes dark for a second. He focuses himself, pulls the speargun into his hands, checks the spear is in place, checks the tautness of the trigger – he built this speargun himself when he was working up north and needed something to occupy his evenings while his subordinates painted the town ale-coloured – and pulls the elastic band back around the end of the spear. The gun is loaded. He holds it by its handle and stalks forward. The water is grey and pinpricked with pebbles and seaweed. Above the water, the sun is careening around the other side of the cloud. The sun glimmers off something in the water. It catches his eye and makes him hesitate for a second, just a second.

The bass crosses from about six feet in front of him, from right to left. He squares up his speargun, takes aim and depresses the trigger feeling the jolt of the spear leaving the gun. He closes his eyes.

There are some things he cannot control.

JAMES WALL

DANCING TO NAT KING COLE

CHARLES AND KATHERINE Simpson are finishing their breakfast when the telephone rings. He starts to rise from the kitchen table but then stops and looks quizzical, as if he's forgotten something, and returns to his scrambled egg.

Katherine places her hand on his shoulder as she leaves the table. In the hallway, she picks up the phone, black and heavy in her palm. Rebecca wants to know if they're free for lunch.

'That'll be lovely, dear.' She rearranges her hair in the mirror, sighs, and then peers in closer; her eyes look dark and puffy. 'No later than 12pm, mind. Your father gets restless and over-tired.'

'Katherine,' he calls from the kitchen. She detects a sprinkle of worry in his voice. It's there more and more nowadays.

'I'm on the phone,' she says, holding her hand over the mouthpiece, and then releasing it. 'I'd better go. See you later.'

'Katherine!'

She pauses before returning to the kitchen, and then carries on through. He nods to his plate.

'Very nice that, my love.'

'Rebecca's coming for lunch,' she says.

'Lovely,' says Charles. 'What's on the goggle-box?'

He calls her to join him as he makes his way to the living room. He'll sit down in his cream leather chair opposite the TV. She'll sit on the sofa next to him soon and they'll hold hands across the arm, as usual.

She slowly chews her rasher of bacon in the quiet before the TV volume in the living room increases and she can hear every word of the news. She closes her eyes and breathes in slowly and deeply, and then reaches for her cup of tea. It's barely warm but she knows he'll ask for another in a minute. Her breakfast cup is white with pink blossoms. There was another but he broke it; she can't remember how. It'll come to her later.

Rebecca smiles broadly at the doorway, her arms outstretched, and she kisses her mother, and then her father.

'You should have told us you were coming,' he says. 'We're going out for lunch.'

'She can always join us,' says Katherine.

'Excellent,' he says.

The leaves have turned orange and yellow, and are gathering on the lawn and the pavement. There was a young lad who used to clear them for £2 but she's not seen him for some time.

As Charles goes to open the garage door, Rebecca takes his arm and guides him to her car. She and Katherine sold his Mercedes some time ago, and they take taxis now when it's just the two of them.

'I want to chauffeur you today, Daddy,' she says.

He raises his eyebrows and a slight smirk spreads across his face.

'If you insist.' He raises a finger in the air. 'As it's you.'

Katherine winks at Rebecca as he slowly climbs into the passenger seat, and then sits in the back.

'Seat belt, Dad.'

He waves his hand dismissively. 'Drive on,' he says.

Katherine catches Rebecca's eye in the rear view mirror and nods to carry on.

At The Angel, the waiter shows them to their usual table by the open fire. Charles orders Whitebait and a bottle of Chablis.

'I haven't decided what I'm having yet, Dad,' says Rebecca, but Katherine places her hand on her arm to quieten her. She orders the plaice.

'I need the toilet,' he says, and looks to Katherine.

'You remember where it is.' She gestures to the far end of the bar.

For a second his eyebrows raise, as if in surprise, and she wonders if he remembers coming here before. 'Of course,' he says.

On their own, Rebecca asks how they are.

Katherine's eyes fall. 'Fine,' she says.

'Really? He seems worse than last time.'

She tells her of their days, how after all these years they still get up together in the morning and sit in the kitchen with their tea, how they watch TV together, read the paper together.

She doesn't tell Rebecca that he follows her around the house and calls her name if left alone for a minute, how he clears away unfinished plates from the table and piles them in the dishwasher, or sometimes turns it on with nothing inside. He cleans the kitchen surfaces over and over again and constantly tidies the house, often putting things in the wrong place. He gets angry if she questions him and so she keeps quiet. She stays longer in the bathroom than she needs, until he calls her, when she knows she has to return.

'He's a bit tired today,' she says, repeatedly glancing over to the Gents. 'He'll have a sleep later I'm sure.'

'You make him sound like a baby.' Rebecca's smile shrinks

as Katherine holds her eye. 'Sorry.' She pauses. 'You look tired.'

'I'm fine. We're both fine.'

Rebecca reaches for her arm, and squeezes it through Katherine's pink jacket. Her grip is tighter than she expects and Katherine snatches her arm away, at once conscious of her clothes hanging loosely from her. She turns towards the toilets.

'Ah, here he is.'

Charles is making his way back to their table, steadying himself on the bar as he hums 'Unforgettable'. On rainy Sunday afternoons, he used to put the record player on in the living room and they would dance to Nat King Cole.

She notices a dark patch the size of a Satsuma on his beige trousers by his crotch, and hopes that Rebecca hasn't seen it. She dips her head and stares at the knot of wood in the table.

Later, when the waiter is clearing away their plates, he asks if everything was alright.

'Lovely,' says Katherine, looking down at her half-eaten fishcake. 'Just couldn't manage it all.' She hasn't felt hungry for a while now.

Charles asks for a brandy.

'I don't think that's a good idea,' says Katherine.

'Let's get a cuppa at home, Dad,' adds Rebecca.

When the brandy arrives, he raises his eyebrows and smiles cheekily. He swirls it around the glass and sniffs at it before taking a sip. Putting the glass down, he reaches into his jacket pocket for a packet of Dunhill and takes one out.

'It's no smoking, Dad.'

'Nonsense. Where's my lighter?' He pats his pockets, finds it and lights the cigarette. Swirls of smoke drift wispily around his head.

'You can't smoke in here,' says Katherine.

He drags on the cigarette and exhales. He never takes in any of the smoke and sits in a plume of grey mist. Flecks of ash land on his chest.

The waiter comes over to the table. 'There's no smoking, I'm afraid, sir.'

'No smoking? Whoever heard of such a thing?'

The waiter glances to Katherine and then returns to Charles. 'I'm sorry, but you will need to put it out.'

'Put it out?'

'Please, Charles. You don't really want it anyway.' She puts her hand on his knee.

The waiter waits, Charles takes another drag and reaches forward to the table.

'There's no ashtray,' he says.

'The waiter will take it for you,' says Katherine, looking up at him.

She watches him take the cigarette away and thinks of their visit here the previous week when he tried to smoke then too. At the restaurant door, Katherine stops and lets the others carry on to the car as she turns to look back at their table. It's clear except for the brandy glass, barely touched. The waiter returns to clear it away.

At home, Rebecca helps her mother make the tea. Charles is in the living room, the TV on loud.

'Can you turn it down, Dad?' she says, carrying in the tray. She puts it on the coffee table, and passes him a cup. 'Can't hear ourselves think.'

He points the remote at the TV and presses down quickly. A green bar appears on the screen but only moves slightly.

They sit on the sofa.

'That's not much quieter,' says Rebecca.

'He won't wear his aid,' says Katherine.

'It's so loud. It can't do your ears any good.'

'What?' she says, and they laugh. Katherine feels a lightness in her stomach and can't stop giggling.

'I'm trying to watch this,' says Charles.

They both toss their heads back, tears trickling down their cheeks. He shakes his head and turns the volume up higher.

After a while, their laughter subsides and soon Katherine notices him snoring.

'Can't believe he can sleep in this noise,' says Rebecca. Katherine reaches over to prise the remote from his fingers and turns it down.

Upstairs, Rebecca helps her mother make the beds.

'You should get a cleaner,' she says, flicking the duvet on his bed.

'I can manage. Besides, it would just confuse him to have someone else here.'

In the bathroom, they separate the whites and colours from the washing basket and put them into two piles.

'Hark!' Katherine says, her finger in the air.

'I didn't hear anything.'

'I'll check on him and put the kettle on,' she says.

His mouth is open and his head is on one side. She often watches him when he's asleep and doesn't mind his snoring. He's like he used to be then.

His sleep becomes more erratic, and increasingly he gets up in the middle of the night and dresses, shaking her awake too. In the kitchen at 4am with his coat on, he asks when they're going out. Then he looks lost, as if wondering what he's doing up at this time. Sometimes, he goes back to bed. Other times, she battles to occupy him until lunchtime. They eat out most days, at the same few familiar restaurants. He sleeps when they get home, if she's lucky.

A month after their lunch with Rebecca, Katherine is hoovering upstairs in the afternoon while he sleeps in his chair.

It's an effort to push and pull it along the landing and it doesn't pick up all the bits from the carpet. At the top of the stairs, she hears his voice above its drone and turns it off.

She finds him in his study.

'Where is it?' His voice is as hard as steel.

'What're you looking for? I thought you were asleep.'

'Gladstone,' he says, as he gestures to the bookshelf in his study. 'Who's taken my bloody book?'

His anger makes her start, like tasting sour milk. She traces a line across the books in front of her but isn't really looking. She likes it best when she's alone in here, amongst the smell of wood and the faint trace of his aftershave. There's a small residue of it left in a bottle in the bathroom that she keeps meaning to throw away.

She shakes her head and says she can't see the book. The phone rings and she hurries to the hallway. Rebecca wants to chat, but Katherine suspects she's just bored. She offers for her to stay with them.

'Could go for lunch,' she says. 'Or just have a natter on the sofa.'

Rebecca says she'll come over soon.

'Your father's calling,' Katherine says. 'I'll have to go.'

'Oh,' says Rebecca. 'So soon? I wanted to talk.'

'We will,' says Katherine.

Charles is quiet now.

'I'll ring you later.'

The shelves are empty in the study, the books now on the floor around the desk in the centre, and Charles isn't there. She finds him sitting in his chair in the living room, a cigarette in between his fingers and smoke drifting from his mouth.

'Did you find it?' she asks.

'What?'

'The book.'

'What book? What are you talking about, woman?'

Ash drops from his cigarette onto the carpet.

'Charles,' she says. 'Be careful.' On her knees at his feet, she tries to cup the ash into her palm without smudging the carpet.

As she stands up, he leans over to the small table next to him and stubs the cigarette out in the ashtray. He picks up the *Telegraph* and then reaches for another cigarette.

'You've just had one, darling,' she says.

He looks up at her, the packet in his hand. 'Who are you?'

She feels aware of her arms, how they dangle stupidly by her sides. 'It's me,' she whispers.

'How did you get in here? Where's Katherine?' His eyes are narrow and darker than normal. They can't seem to focus on her properly. 'Well?' he shouts. 'What've you done with my wife?'

As he pulls himself up from the chair, she turns and walks towards the door. She looks behind her and he shoos her on with his hand, like cattle. 'Go on, away, away.'

In the hallway, she hurries into the study, closing the door behind her, and crawls under the desk. She listens to his feet shuffle slowly along the parquet floor outside the room and then stop. 'Katherine,' he shouts, but she keeps quiet. The sound of his footfall recedes as he climbs the stairs and he calls out to her again.

It's quiet now under the desk and she breathes easier.

Then she hears Charles cry out, and there are bangs and thumps down the stairs, over and over, getting louder and louder. She shoves her fingers in her ears and scrunches up her eyes, lowering her back until she's in a small ball.

She's not sure how long she stays like this but it feels like hours. Slowly, she removes her fingers and it's silent. The smells of wood and floor polish rise up. The telephone rings, echoing round the hallway, spreading throughout the house, calling to her, but she makes no move to answer it. In her mind, she sees the bathroom, her toothbrush in the glass by the mirror, the bedroom with her bed neatly made. Her breakfast cup and saucer are on the kitchen table, and the clock ticks on the wall above it. In the living room, a thin line of smoke is rising from the last of the cigarette as the phone continues to ring. And then it stops.

NINA KILLHAM

MY WIFE THE HYENA

I AM NOT a bad man. I work every weekday until six. I keep a tidy desk and leave it every night devoid of clutter. I have worked my way up to my own office with a window. It overlooks the parking lot where my four-door sedan awaits. Bought with my first and only merit raise.

I am a family man. Of course. With three children whom I suspect I love. And a wife who has a steady part-time job which allows for the occasional trip to our caravan by the sea.

I keep my office door open though no one ever thinks to visit. I don't know why. Busy people with busy lives, I suppose. But every evening I look up from my papers and listen to my colleagues call to each other when they head out to the corner pub.

During the yearly office party, my wife and I stand on the periphery, stiff drinks in hand, alone. My wife, I can feel her tense by my side. She is not like the other wives, who are younger, prettier and usually on the other side of the cavernous room. Because they avoid us, me and my wife. As if she is catching.

Maybe I'm used to it. Her distinctive canine look, her ears twitching, her mouth emitting sharp yaps.

We're all used to it. Our children find it perfectly normal to be held by the scruff of the neck.

Chloe doesn't bat an eye when her mother barrels into her for refusing to do her homework. My wife clutches at her throat with her fangs until my daughter acquiesces. Chloe just brushes herself off, refuses to look her mother in the eye and bounds into the hall to fetch her book bag.

It was unfortunate that my boss was once there to witness the struggle. The one time he agreed to come over for a drink. The man had been helping himself to hummus and pita but his bite remained unchewed in his mouth at the shock.

What are you staring at? Emma – that's my wife – growled as she padded past.

The word must have gotten out because the next morning I saw their smiles, one part sympathy, three parts smirk.

And yes, it's uncomfortable. This is, after all, my office. The place I go to every day. I am in 8.30 sharp and listen as the others stumble in. I see their smiles flashed to each other as I walk past at noon on my way to buy a sandwich. The low Grrrr the head one emits.

They don't see her the way I do.

They don't know that alone in my office, I can't stop thinking of her. Sitting at my desk I find myself dreaming about the way her large tongue hangs dripping when she lies on the bed in a pant. You see, she is everything I want in a wife. Can those men in the other offices say that?

Every night she reads to the twins, letting the two children lean back against her flanks. Jessie likes to hold her tail and stroke it. Emma flicks it away when it gets too rough.

In the meantime, I go to the bathroom to brush my teeth. I take one condom out of the pack and slide it under my pillow. And then watch her come to bed with anticipation.

Most nights she trots in, noses shut the door and opens her large mouth wide in a protracted yawn. Her eyes are rimmed with black, her nose wet and glistening. I lie in bed, covers to my chin, and watch her. She jumps up and flops onto the bed and noses her privates, licking and picking. I try to turn my eyes away. But can't get away from the sound of the slurping. I feel aroused.

She always turns three times then flops down, groaning, with her nose on the pillow.

Emma, I'll whisper.

No response. I'll lift my head and look over. And she'll be fast asleep.

Sometimes I'll put my hand on her shoulder and give it a little shake. The low growl is unmistakable. My hand jerks back. And I'll watch as her mottled tongue swings itself over her nose again. She settles back into sleep. The sound of her deep breathing actually calms me. And we'll both slumber deeply, sometimes with my hand on her flank, completely at peace.

Some nights I get lucky.

And today is my birthday.

As I tidy my desk to go home, I think briefly of the usual cards I expect from the children – bought by their mother and scrawled indifferently with their names. I think of the hastily wrapped electrical gadget – invariably the wrong one – from my wife. And the tight, endless call from the great aunt who raised me.

But mainly I think about my birthday treat.

Which is why it's so difficult today to concentrate on work. All day my thoughts have drifted home. I sit here and catch whiffs of her scent.

Her cooking is never memorable. It is difficult to cook with four paws. And tonight will be no exception.

After the store-bought cake is eaten, crumbs licked clean, the children will race away. I will gaze with lager-glazed eyes over the kitchen table to where my wife sits, furry ears pricked, her black liquid eyes bright. I will watch as she laughs, as she does most nights, at me, her spotted haunches shaking with mirth.

Upstairs my children will squabble. But I will look around my kitchen, the kitchen I pay for by sitting in my office every day for the last 15 years, and see my wife's footprints leading from the door, still muddy and wet. I will listen to her pad around the kitchen, nosing closed the dishwasher, her toenails clicking on the linoleum floor. I will follow her up the stairs.

I will wait for her, naked, the sheets up to my chin. And I will think of my empty office and of my dismissive colleagues and of their difficult wives. I've caught glimpses of the tails dragging beneath their dresses. The spots their make-up fails to completely conceal.

These colleagues know it's my birthday. The secretary has pointedly passed along a card for them to sign. I look at their signatures, some big and bold, others small and severely slanted.

Later when the hours draw to a close I can hear them talking, no doubt wondering if they should invite me, just this once. But the head one mumbles something that produces a loud guffaw. I hear them crowd into the elevator together and listen as the doors close.

But it doesn't matter. Really. I would have said no anyway.

It is my birthday and my wife is planning something nice.

I hurry home, leaving their card propped up on my desk.

They act as if I don't exist.

But I do exist. I certainly do.

I am not some joke to be mumbled with a rolled eye, fag in hand and a freshly drawn pint on the table.

Because they know. They know. They've only got to hear their wives laugh, haven't they?

CHARLES BOYLE

BUDAPEST

IN THE KITCHEN, which is the room where they eat, an ancient peasant cat, no fancy breed, is lying awkwardly on a chair and panting, though the day is cold. No one is paying it attention. Beyond the window are clouds, fields, the kind of view people call uninterrupted.

He is trespassing, he has no right to be here, and it feels like freedom.

'The wood across the valley is the largest in the county,' James announces from the other end of the table, as if he had planted every tree himself.

'There are wolves,' C says quietly, looking at him, teasing.

'They bay to the moon,' he says.

'They do more than that.'

'Is it OK?' asks the woman called Marcia. 'Should we get it some water or something?'

She's worrying about the cat, and he is wary of the drift. If anyone asks if he has animals of his own, he'll say no. He has no affinity with dumb creatures. And yet just this week he has yielded to pressure – family pressure, normality pressure: he was cornered – and purchased a pair of rabbits for his pair of children. They squat, shivering with fear, or hunger. How is he to know? Their droppings are hard brown beads.

The cat is ill. It is a fuse easily lit, after so much wine and loosening of voices. James, C's husband, is intent on spending a large amount of money on an operation to prolong its life. Let it go, C says, as if pushing it to the side of her plate. Anything else is selfishness, not love. He wants to spend that money for himself, truth be told. Take the cat in and bring it back hurt, bewildered, pawing at its shaved and mangled body, or take it in unknowing and put it down. A good life come to term, and no suffering. *That* is mercy.

He knows it is her marriage she is talking about. Everything here – the hand-painted plates on the dresser, the photographs, the scribbled lists and numbers of emergency plumbers – is a stage set, history, disposable. Excitement makes him tremble. He wants to turn to whoever is sitting next to him, which happens to be Marcia, and hug her. He knows that if anyone says even the weakest thing funny, he is danger of laughing too loud.

'I'm sorry,' C says, standing up. Lighter than skin, the folds of her dress cascade; he still has the ghost of it on his fingers from when they came in. She has, he's noticed, a way of widening her eyes after speaking; she is not apologising at all. 'Really, you shouldn't be listening to this. Who wants more wine?'

Marcia puts her hand over the rim of her glass, as if she's about to perform a conjuring trick. But James does want, pushing his own glass across the table. It occurs to him that James has him down as gay. There were meant to be just four around the table, C and James and Marcia and his brother, Maurice, recently widowed, whom she'd wanted to put together with Marcia, but when she called and his brother had explained that he happened to be staying then of course, why not.

Marcia is a counsellor, with devout opinions. Everything can be explained. Everyone else, to her, is like a pet, dependent. James is a retired lawyer, a former colleague of his brother's; he is, or was, a brilliant mind, his brother has said. C is his fate. A few weeks from now – sooner, sooner – she will turn to him in bed and say: 'James thought you were gay.' He is sure of this.

'Did *you*?'

'He still does.'

Across the street, Marcia is coming out of the village bookshop with Maurice. She turns away, but they have seen her. There is a pause, until the road is clear, and then they are surrounding her with their togetherness, thanking her for the lunch, fumbling with bags, showing her what they have bought in the bookshop. She is not surprised.

Maurice has sprained his wrist. He parades his bandage. He was putting the lawnmower back in the shed; he slipped, he fell, he put out a hand to save himself, and now this. For all that he is a lawyer, it's a wonder he didn't electrocute himself too. Men are so helpless. He can't even work a tin-opener. Marcia is cooking for him.

'He did everything, for years and years,' Marcia says. She means for Alice, Maurice's wife, who is dead, who died of complications. She was alcoholic, everyone knows this.

'And really, it's bloody difficult,' Marcia goes on. She is gleeful, victorious. 'He's so stubborn. He's given so much he's forgotten how to take. It's the harder thing, of course, but just as important. We're starting from scratch.'

She has known Marcia for a decade, longer. She is happy for her. She hadn't conceived that life could be so simple.

'She's a good teacher,' says Maurice, a schoolboyish gleam in his eyes that takes her aback. He likes his food.

The eyes, yes, and other small things too – the way he tilts his head to the left when he's listening – though there is little obvious physical resemblance between the brothers, nothing you'd notice at first glance. She suspects that they get on but they are not close, these brothers. They see things in each other that they don't like about themselves, they are happy to stay out of range. Brotherhood: the roles assumed, the competition, one pitching camp where the other leaves space unguarded.

Maurice is still looking at her, awaiting a blessing.

She is beginning to think like Marcia, to analyse, which is a form of helplessness. She looks over Maurice's shoulder: the street, the weathered stone buildings, the shopkeepers who chat and ask questions and tot up little sums; and then the green hills, as still as on the picture postcards. The names on the village war memorial – Atkinson, Hancock, Smith, Weatherspoon – are a mantra that holds this place in its grip. She met Alice only twice, maybe three times. Once at a law society dinner. There had been a point at which she'd been completely beautiful. Her glance was withering. It was a long marriage; there are children somewhere, out in the world, Hong Kong, Australia. The weather is mild, changeable. At the weekend it will be hot. The traffic on this street gets worse every year. Marcia and Maurice head off towards the post office, her hand cupping his elbow.

She has a flat in town – really it is her husband's flat, James's, there are law books in glass-fronted bookcases, but since he retired it's almost never used. He wakes in her bed to the sound of shouting voices and the screech of tyres. A fight in the street, he thinks. Grey light, sometime around dawn. Naked, he walks through to the living room and finds her sitting cross-legged on the floor, watching a film on TV. He strokes her hair. Not moving her head, she pats the floor for him to sit beside her. Together they watch two women driving fast through small towns, on the run. She will watch to the end, even though the end is foretold by the music. After half an hour, with the heating still not come on, he sweeps the covering from the sofa and wraps it around them.

Daily, the world reveals more of itself. Sometimes he feels like a tourist in his own city. He talks to strangers. He tells her about the man he met while walking through the park, a man like a gypsy with his hair twisted around the strap at the back of his baseball cap. The man said he was from the north of Sweden, the far north, and he was a poet – would he like to hear a poem? He said he would rather hear a joke. The man told him a long joke, it must have gone on for at least five minutes, entirely in Swedish or some remote dialect from beyond the Arctic Circle, and by the end the man was doubled up, laughing uncontrollably. She laughs too, not just with her face but her toes, her fingers, her belly.

Or he is waiting at the barrier when the train comes in and does its meek slow stop and the doors open and the people file through, the busy ones checking their watches and the old women who have been travelling since the days of porters and the students with their crass but ergonomic backpacks, and he carries on waiting till the platform is bare as a seaside promenade in winter and she isn't there. What she teaches her lovers, he thinks, and not for the first time, is patience.

There are days when there's white cloud all morning and mizzly rain in the afternoon and then at seven in the evening the sky clears to china blue and the sun shines undimmed as if it's never put a foot wrong in its life.

Not patience of the kind that's deemed a virtue (it isn't). There've been times when, heading to her flat, they haven't been able to wait even that long but have ducked into an alleyway and torn at each other's clothing.

He goes home. It would fit better if when he comes in his wife is peeling carrots but she isn't, she's just standing in the kitchen knowing there is a next thing to do but having lost track.

'Did you get the . . . ?' she asks.

'The milk?'

'The milk, yes. We're out.'

'I forgot,' he says. 'I'm sorry.'

From his room at the top of the house where he now sleeps he can see the rabbit cage in the garden, and his younger child sitting cross-legged in front of it. No sign of the rabbits. They are in their hutch, their little room, sulking.

He phones her. He doesn't leave a message.

On the way to the station, he decides, she came across a maimed owl, which needed putting back in one piece. Or just as she was about to leave a friend called her from Romania, or maybe Hungary – which country is Budapest the capital of? – in tears. She has a problem with timetables, with the 24-hour clock. She doesn't wear a watch. Her appetite is limitless and like most people with appetite she is also generous. When he pulls on clothes and says he must go she kicks off the sheets and opens her legs, offering, asking to be kissed, lips to lips.

His son is still there, in front of the rabbits' cage, waiting for them to appear. All day, all night if need be. Where it comes from, this stubbornness, this dedication, he has no idea. He cannot recall when he has been more proud. If this is his son, he cannot be all that bad: this is a way, one of many he knows, of damning himself.

The rabbits, he thinks, have been eaten by a fox – there are plenty around, probably more than where she is, in the countryside – but there is no litter of tufts of fur and bloody scraps. Or they have escaped, are returning to the wild, in which case they will not survive for long.

His phone rings. She tells him she's tired, that today has not been the best of days, that—

'When will I see you?'

She's not sure – the weekend, maybe. She'll come up on Saturday, yes. Saturday early.

'The milk train?' he says. Then he asks after the cat.

There is no cat. The cat disappeared, she says, weeks ago. She has heard of this before: they have some instinct that tells them their time is drawing near, and they go off alone to meet their maker in private.

When he looks out of the window again his son is not there but the rabbits are, out of their hutch and pressed up against the wire. He closes his eyes and sees the wood across the valley, 'the largest in the county'; he enters its shade, its darkness, hears rustlings and flutterings and sudden sharp cries. Though they have done nothing to deserve it – but when was anything decided on merit? – animals have the last word, even the last laugh. They are primed for this, it's in their genetic engineering. The thought is like a mouthful of food that tastes very different from what you'd expected, from what you'd imagined.

A year later she is in Budapest, visiting Hannah. Hand-luggage only, and she still doesn't wear a watch. Instead, on her wrist there is a sequence of numbers, written in biro and starting to smudge. It is a cold afternoon, autumn, but they are eating outside, on a terrace. Life is complicated. Also with them, but not just now at the table, is a Peruvian child, a boy of around six, with flat black hair and eyes so clear and deep she could swim in them.

'Oh, him,' she says, in answer to something Hannah has said. *Him*, in distinction from the other him, James, whom they've been talking about for the past half-hour. It's like being part of a reading group, discussing the characters.

She is holding a stuffed animal, a sheep, which the boy has more than relinquished. He is over there, crouched in a corner of the terrace, exploring. They have been swimming in the pool of an old and expensive hotel that predates the communist era and has come out the other side with surly changing-room attendants untrained in the ways of customer service. She feels lucky to have all her life been free.

Except that she is not free. She feels she is on the set of a film, whether farce or thriller she doesn't yet know. The boy is the adopted child of Hannah and her Hungarian husband; the husband has been cast adrift by Hannah but is determined to climb back on board and has taken to following them around, stalking them. He refuses to drown. Hence the numbers inked on her hand, which she must punch into the alarm system in Hannah's apartment within ten seconds of entering. She scrabbles around in the dark, trying not to panic, imagining that she will be arrested and taken to an underground cellar and interrogated under a blinding light and will have her fingernails slowly pulled out.

'He has wonderful eyes,' she says. And adds, having given herself the cue: 'He has a wonderful cock. Effervescent.'

The boy comes to his mother with a spider cupped in his hands. 'A boy spider or a girl spider?' he wants to know. He speaks English like an American. (This, she has been meaning to say, is why Hannah cannot leave him alone in the apartment while she's at work, alone with the TV tuned to American game-shows; and why she herself cannot abide indoors in that clean, functional but badly windowed flat, where you have to switch on a light even to make breakfast, for more than an hour; why she must take the boy out and thereby condemn herself to the frantic punching of the code on the keypad when they have run out of things to do. But she has only been here for two days.)

'For god's sake,' Hannah says, laughing. She is happy, or believes she is. She delivers a lecture on the good life – Hannah is not unlike Marcia, in her belief that life can be made to fit – while all the time attending to the boy's asking, asking. Why do spiders have so many legs? How long do spiders live? Is this a baby spider or a grown-up?

The couple at the next table are tourists, like herself. German, Dutch? The man is intent on the map at the back of his guidebook, folded out on the table. The woman is looking across the river, so entranced she appears to have forgotten what it is she should be doing with the forkful of food she has raised. Should she put it back on her plate? Or into her body? If so, through which opening?

Now a man is walking towards them: the waiter, or a secret policeman, or Hannah's outcast, desperate husband.

She really doesn't mind which. She sips wine; it's not for her to say. She looks beyond the man to where the woman at the next table is looking, across the river sparkling in the afternoon sunshine.

OK, the boy says, but how does it know it's grown up, why doesn't it just keep on growing more legs?

Sometimes in old films the camera pulls back from the intimate – the kiss, the fight, the horses being saddled – to show the backdrop panorama: the cityscape, its domes and spires and palaces, the snow-capped mountains. How beautiful, you think. And then just as you begin to suspect that it's not for real, that it's a painted backdrop, they cut to the next scene. The budget was tight, you can understand this, it wouldn't stretch to a whole crew staying for months in a luxury scenic location. You can forgive, if there's anything to be forgiven, which there isn't. But not too tight for a painter to paint that landscape, with all the hours of research and the patience of each brushstroke, even though it will be on screen for barely more than a second.

LESLEY GLAISTER

JUST WATCH ME

EXHAUSTED FROM A fit of coughing, he sits hunched over in the bed. She lays her hand between his shoulder blades. The skin is clammy, the pores a field of tiny gasping flowers. When she touches her lips there, the taste is salt. On his right shoulder there's a tattoo, the Chinese character for wisdom he says, but he could have told her anything. How would she know? Years have blurred the design and now it could be a fading bruise, a mesh of broken capillaries, a leak of blood beneath the skin.

'Coming to bed, then?' His tone is tetchy. He strains further forward to peel away from her palm. He reaches for and struggles into his pyjama jacket, shrugging off her attempts to help. He suffers from sweats and chills, and now he's chilly; she can see the pimpling of his skin.

'In a tick,' she says.

He settles back against the pillows, reaches for his book and reading glasses.

'Can I get you anything?' she asks.

He clears his throat, gives her a professorial look from over the specs, and finds his page. He sits motionless in the attitude of one about to read, waiting for her to leave.

In the bathroom she brushes her teeth and unwinds a length of floss. The mirror above the basin is stippled with bits from between his teeth and hers. Disgusting really, if you look at it. The trick is to look through it, which she does as she distorts her face to fossick between her teeth. She sluices her mouth with mouthwash and treats the mirror to an ivory grimace.

Bed then. The cold tap needs fixing, even when you screw it tight it trickles; she should call a plumber. A washer is all it needs. That trickling. Her bare feet contract on the lino as it tickles free a memory. That comically awful room in where was it? Somewhere hot and dissolute. Naples? Venice? You had to go down a flight of dirty stairs to get to the lavatory or shower, but in the bedroom, only inches from the bed, there was a bidet with a trickling tap.

They'd had to avoid each other's eyes as they were shown the room. It was funny, of course, but oddly disturbing. At least it had disturbed Rose.

'It makes sex seem like something dirty,' she said, when the stout, whiskery landlady had left them alone.

'It *is* something dirty,' he said. 'Isn't that the point?'

This was before they were married, before Gina, before the gaps between her teeth or the rubbery folds around her waist.

She'd pulled her dress over her head and stood in her sandals and knickers watching him wriggle out of his jeans. That flat, darkly furred stomach, the tautness of it, always made her catch her breath. His skin was dark against hers, hot against hers, and the sex was dirty there in the stuffy little room. Dirty, but beautiful too.

It was where Gina had been started, though of course they didn't know that till some weeks later. And it was definitely Venice, glittering Venice with its stench of drains.

Afterwards she made him shut his eyes while she squatted, hot feet on the cool marble and squirted a jet of water onto her swollen flesh. As she dabbed herself dry, she noticed that his eyes weren't quite shut, that he was watching through his lashes.

'I told you not to look!' she said.

'I love to watch when you don't know.'

She stepped into her knickers and his eyes followed them up her legs.

'Don't stare.'

She turned away to put on her dress. She'd bought the dress especially for this holiday - pale blue cotton, halter-necked to show her shoulders off. That her shoulders were the loveliest part of her was her own and private opinion - especially when lightly tanned. She'd have liked to make herself look nice - to primp a bit - in private. It made her self-conscious that he was sprawled there, quite relaxed in his nakedness, hands behind his head, watching her every move. She brushed her hair hard and pulled it back - a little too tightly - in a rubber band.

'Let's go for a beer,' he said and yawned and stretched luxuriously. 'God, I love holidays.'

They walked in silence to a pavement café and he ordered beer and she a cup of tea. All the shaded spots had gone and they had to sit in the full glare of the sun. He was wearing a white shirt and looked darkly devastating. She saw a woman gawping at him from another table and felt both annoyed and proud. The skin on the back of her neck began to tighten in the sun and she let down her hair to cover it. The tea was disappointing, a bag floating in warm water. She had only chosen it to make some sort of obscure point, and she eyed his coolly beaded glass of lager enviously.

'So, what's up then?' he asked, in a tone of exaggerated patience.

'You promised not to look,' she said.

'You're not still sulking over that! Christ! You should be glad I want to look.'

'How do you like being stared at?' She dropped a greenish sliver of lemon into her cup.

'Doesn't bother me.'

'Even if I watched you doing something private?'

'You can watch me do anything you like.'

'Anything?'

He lit a cigarette, inhaled deeply, leant back and extended his crossed legs. It was like a challenge.

'Have a shit?' she whispered pathetically.

He hooted. 'If you want.' He raised his eyebrows. '*Do* you want?'

'Of course not!' Blushing, she gulped her tea.

They sat in silence and she watched him watch other women flaunt past, until he said: 'Remind me, Rose. *What* are we arguing about?'

'Nothing.' Aware of the eyes of the other woman on him, she leaned forward to touch his knee and he smiled, believing himself forgiven. No not forgiven, in his opinion there was nothing to forgive, but believing she'd got over her silly tizz.

Now she switches on the shower, undoes her dressing gown. She notices mould on the shower-curtain; you can get a spray for that. It gets harder to lift her leg over the side of the bath but she does it and stands under the warm, irregular sprinkle of water. Get a power-shower, Gina says. Gina picks holes when she comes home now – *get a this, get a that* – and brings rubber gloves with her. However did they spawn such a clean-freak child, and out of that lovely dirtiness?

Although it's bed time, she lets her hair get wet. She lathers her body with gardenia soap, enjoying the fragrance, the slickness of her skin. One day she'll cut her toe-nails, but not tonight. Tonight they are too far away.

'Watch you do *anything?*' she challenged later, after a bottle of wine.

'Anything.'

His eyes were so dark then, with such a spark. Dark light you'd say if that wasn't nonsense. That holiday they were at it all the time, but she never used the bidet in the room again, preferring to wrap herself in his musky shirt and go downstairs to wash in private. He didn't care. He would even kneel and pee in the bidet, only a couple of feet from her head. And later, as he slept, she'd lie and listen to the trickle of the leaky tap, like something silver running through the night.

Can't go to bed with dripping hair, she'll soak the pillow and wake up a fright. She turbans her hair in a towel, puts on her dressing gown and pours a little brandy, just a teeny one. Brandy on a Tuesday night. Decadent; whatever would Gina say? She swigs it down. Tastes vile along alongside the mint of mouthwash – but it's cheering. Is it Tuesday, after all?

The gas-fire lights with a gasp of surprise – this time of night! She kneels before it, teasing out the tangles, allowing the orange glow to warm and dry her hair. The bones in her knees press uncomfortably against the rug, an old stained thing that still smells of the last dog – and he died years ago. She sighs. Get a new one – rug not dog. Sometimes Gina has a point. There are teak shelves running up either side of the fireplace and on each a dusty treasure that has been there years: souvenirs, framed photographs, and at the bottom, something she'd forgotten, a pebble painted to look like a snail. Rose fishes it out and weighs it in her hand. Gina painted this for Eric for Fathers' Day, when she was 7 or 8, and he used it as a paperweight. Rose smiles at the clever way it's painted, very precise and almost life-like – very Gina. And then she puts the pebble back.

He never hid the evidence. When she found the note it was folded under this paperweight. She was in his study, dusting maybe, or just poking around, and had lifted the paperweight to admire it – not seeing the note at first.

And then the paper, smart blue Basildon Bond, caught her eye.

Idly, she picked it up and read.

You fool. Dear fool. How can something that's so wrong feel so right? Here's your other cuff-link. Do be careful! Before too long . . . Pxxx

She read it twice. There was only one thing it could possibly mean. And he'd put it under Gina's paperweight. That was the worst thing, seemed, ridiculously, the worst thing in that first moment of knowing. And because she couldn't bear the note to touch Gina's work of art, she left it unfolded and un-weighed down, which he might have noticed. But if he did, he never said.

It was around this time that he started doing 'over-time' and what a cliché. She felt almost sorry for him when he came back with his excuses, hardly excuses at all, excuses so lame they needed zimmer frames to help them through the door.

'You're late,' she remarked one night, looking up from the news.

'Am I?'

'Work?'

'Sort of, got held up with a . . . thing.' He looked ruffled, stubbly, tired. By then he'd started wearing specs and the light reflecting in them hid the beauty of his eyes, his hair was growing thin, his stomach soft, but *someone* fancied him.

She was quite impressed by that. Not just impressed but terrified; not just terrified but riveted.

Someone beginning with P: Pauline? Penelope? Patricia? She didn't know anyone beginning with P who was the least bit likely. When she did the laundry she examined his clothes for traces. He was having sex with P, she could tell this from the curious wrong tang of his underwear. Once she found a curly auburn hair caught in the weave of a sock. Often she would catch the edge of perfume – a heavy sophisticated musk or crushed orchid smell – certainly nothing like her own fresh and simple eau de rose.

And then, one day, quite by accident, she saw him – saw them. On a Saturday morning, after a furtively taken phone call, he claimed he had to go into the office to sort out some emergency, but would be home by six at the latest. They had people coming for dinner and he promised to be there to set the table, open the wine; *all the difficult stuff*, she'd muttered.

She saw him enter the Goat and Thistle. At least, she thought so, not absolutely certain at first. She'd caught a sloping shoulder, a jacket the right shade of green, but the glimpse had been too quick for her to be sure.

What had taken her to town that day? Hair, was it her hair? It must have been her hair. She walked past the pub and turned the corner – yes, it must have been her hair; the salon was down that cobbled street. But there was time before her appointment and she had turned back, passed the pub once more. The door swung open on her third perambulation belching beery air and smoke. She could do with using the Ladies, she thought, and why not have a snack there? It was lunchtime, after all. Going into a pub alone was not something she had ever done, but there was no law against it.

The interior was gloomy and dominated by the flashing neon of games machines – Kerang – Lucky Strike – Gold Rush. The bar was L-shaped with booths of seats and tables and stools along the bar. She wore a breezy preoccupied expression; if she ran into him she was ready to express surprise. If he turned out to be alone, she'd join him; if he were not alone, as he was likely not to be – what then? She gulped in a breath and went to the bar.

'Yup?' the youngster behind it said. He was chewing gum and she winced at the squelch of it.

'Small shandy,' she said, picked up the curling laminated menu, and chose at random. 'And a cheese and onion roll.'

'Right,' he said, and snapped his gum. 'Sit down, I'll bring it over.'

The leatherette seats in the empty booth looked sticky. She peered round the corner to where the dartboard and lavatory entrances were. More empty tables there – she took a step and then she saw the back of Eric's head. He was facing away from her, in one of the booths. Opposite was P or at least Rose assumed it was P. Her heart did a frantic stutter and she turned, looked at the door. Should she flee? Why had she ordered cheese and onion when it was bound to repeat on her all day? She could do with a brandy rather than a shandy. What was she doing? What on earth did she think she was doing?

She forced in a breath. It was all right. Unless he turned, he would not see her. And P did not know her. She looked terrifying. Her hair was auburn, thick, upswept, and her lips darkly glossed. Of course she was younger, maybe fifteen years Rose's junior, but in sophistication she seemed older, intimidatingly, maturely female. You couldn't say she was beautiful and certainly not pretty, but she was all woman, attractive, sexy woman. And she was actual.

She was leaning across the table towards Eric, talking intently. She had lines between her brows, arched brows, professionally plucked or waxed. Her skin had a proper made-up finish. She looked tended. Someone who took care of herself.

Rose turned to leave. Nothing lost. She hadn't even paid – but here came the youth with the roll on a tray, thick shards of onion protruding from white pap.

'Here?' he said, indicating a seat at a table.

'No here.' Rose pointed to one of the booths, from where she'd be less obtrusive but could continue to watch. She took a step towards the booth – that dark red, sticky seating – and she had to clutch the edge of the table, made unsteady suddenly by the thought of biting into all that onion. 'I don't feel . . . '

Alarmed, the youth banged down the tray, looked for help towards the bar where there was nobody to help. He took her arm steered her to the seat. 'You all right?' he said.

'Just a . . . ' she murmured.

'Can I get you anything else?' he said. 'An aspirin p'raps?'

He was a sweet boy, she saw. She forced her lips into a smile. 'It's all right,' she mumbled, 'thank you, I'll be all right in a minute.'

She sat and watched the bubbles crawl up the sides of her glass. One of the machines blurted out a fanfare followed by the chunter of coins. She turned to watch an elderly man shovel them into his jacket pockets; he did it in a feral surreptitious way and immediately started feeding them in again. He had hairs like stuffing coming out of his nose and the machine made his flesh flash red, yellow, green. This was the sort of pub Eric would refer to as 'hole in the wall'; not the sort of place they went to together, on holiday say, not the sort of place any of their acquaintances would be likely to frequent; he would think himself quite safe.

P got up and Rose put her head down, catching only a pair of pointed boots with sharpish little heels that clacked as she walked past. Rose flexed her toes in her own scuffed loafers. Eric hadn't moved. Once P had passed, Rose leant out to have a better look. She was wearing a short jacket and skirt suit – and her hips were disproportionately wide, thighs solid under a nylon sheen. Something to get hold of, would be Eric's opinion, she could almost hear him say it. Rose was a slight, small bosomed person, with bitten nails and straggly eyebrows. What a contrast he was having.

She picked the onion out of her roll and took a bite of bread and cheese, which tasted strongly of margarine. The food wadded itself against the roof of her mouth and she had to swallow hard to send it down. She took a sip of shandy; and stood to go. As she passed the bar, P turned and Rose caught the expression in her eyes, all flirty bright and bold – and fixed on Eric.

The air outside had a new bite to it, and the daylight, after the dim interior, seemed shimmery and reckless. She was late for her appointment but didn't apologise. She had her hair cut shorter than ever before, and sipped strong sweet coffee to try to stop the trembling of her hands.

At the dinner party that night she drank too much, laughed too loudly and burned the *boeuf en croute*. Their friends left early, looking quite alarmed. And when they'd gone, she took a rather startled Eric to bed. It was interesting to see his body, to feel him in action, as a stranger would. As P did. What did *she* see in him? What did they do together? How did Rose compare?

Afterwards, they sat up in bed, each with their book. His the biography of a Labour politician, hers a novel.

'Thought I saw you today,' she remarked, idly turning an unread page.

'Unlikely,' he said, without looking up.

'In town – I was in for my hair.'

'It's nice,' he said. 'Takes years off.'

'You think so? What if I dyed it red?'

He frowned and went on reading.

She nursed the affair as if it was her child. After Gina there had been miscarriages and a full-term stillbirth, a boy, dark-haired, firm browed and terribly, utterly still. A boy that Eric wouldn't have mentioned, a boy that had left an empty twitchy sensation in Rose's arms for all those years.

She tried not to become obsessed with the affair, but it was a hobby of a sort, an interest. It was a project. She wanted it to run its course and then to end. Like a dog let off the lead to roam in the park, Eric was allowed this adventure, providing, like a dog, he came home when it was over.

Rose made it easy for him. She never quizzed him about his lateness, or why he'd suddenly become indispensable in the office on Saturdays. She never asked him why he smelled wrong. She'd take his clothes from the washing hamper and bury her nose there trying to give a name to the smell – it wasn't frankly sexual, more mucky sweet – digestive biscuit and hamster cage was the nearest she could get – and always a trace of that heavy perfume. She found theatre tickets in his wallet once; she found the receipt for a lavish cookery book. That hurt. Rose was a damn fine cook, Eric liked to say, and she hated to think herself rivalled in that area; it seemed more of a betrayal for him to enjoy another woman's food than to sleep with her. And he can rarely actually have slept with her. Maybe a ten-minute post-coital doze, but never the journey of a full night.

Not until Brighton anyway. Every year for the past decade he'd taken Rose along to the annual conference – many of his colleagues took their wives or husbands. There were dinners in the evening and over the years she'd made friends with other spouses, during they day they'd shop and lunch and swim together. And after the conference, when all the others had gone, Rose and Eric got into the habit of staying on for a day or two, just lazing, making love in the afternoons, spending time together, romantic time. A dirty weekend he called it, though it was never the weekend. But it would usually be dirty enough in its way, for her anyway, if not, maybe, for him.

And then that year – the year of P – he said, casually over dinner, 'I thought you might give the conference a miss this year. There's been cut-backs and I know the others aren't going – Matt's wife; Peter's wife. It's a pared down affair, a shame but there you are.'

She can remember looking down at her pale blue dinner plate, the slice of quiche half eaten, the innocent new potatoes, the tomatoes in their peppered oil, the pooling green of that oil soaking into the pastry as she waited for her expression to obey her.

'I might come anyway,' she said when she was able to raise her eyes. 'We can still have our time.' She took a mouthful of the quiche but her throat had closed up and it clumped damp and inert on her tongue as he continued, with smooth confidence:

'Let's wait till the end of the month, shall we? Have a proper holiday instead?'

She hadn't answered and he'd taken that as yes. Rose had checked that it was the same hotel, and by phoning Peter's wife had ascertained that his lie was just that, an utter lie. There were no cut-backs, other spouses would be there. Other spouses and P, of course.

When he returned from the conference she washed his clothes and didn't ask him how it went. But she did begin to check his diary. On Wednesday, after the list of meetings, there was scrawled a 'P'. And on Wednesday Eric came home late and weary. In bed Rose sniffed his shoulder and caught the scent of unfamiliar soap. The following Monday, he had jotted 'P' again. By 5.30 Rose was waiting outside the office. She wore a raincoat, far too large, borrowed from a neighbour and had tied a headscarf over her hair. It wasn't much of a disguise and, of course, had Eric bothered to look he'd have recognised her. If he did, she was ready to say she was just passing, and what about a drink? But stopping him wasn't her purpose.

She waited in a doorway across the road from his office exit. It was a blowy day and rubbish tangled round her feet. The wind was nasty, sharp edged, the sort that can blow tears from your eyes. He came out at 6.30, head down, preoccupied, and hurried away. She followed him to a small hotel; of course it would be a hotel. Just before 7, P arrived, the wind messing her hair, her fur collar pulled tight around her throat. P stepped into the revolving door and so, one revolution behind her, did Rose.

The lobby was bright with mirrors and pale furniture and on the reception desk a bowl of green apples gleamed as if polished. P went to the reception desk and Rose went too. She stood beside P and saw, with a frisson of alarm, that her wedding finger was empty. Her nails were dangerous curves of vermilion and Rose scrunched her own bitten nails into her palms.

'I'm meeting Mr Thomas,' P said. Rose winced. He could at least have used a pseudonym.

A smooth-faced girl looked in the register. 'Room 12, lift to your left,' she said.

'Do you have a brochure?' Rose said, standing, perhaps, a bit too close. 'I'm thinking of staying.'

'Excuse me,' P said and stepped round her.

'Do I know you?' Rose asked her.

P's eyes were hazel, her lashes clumpy black; her front teeth were square and lipstick smudged, the smell of fur and perfume coming off her was almost sickening. She looked less polished, not as perfect this close to, nor as intimidatingly poised. 'I do not think so,' she said. She had an accent of some kind; Spanish was it? 'Please excuse me.' She went towards the lift and Rose hastened to the stairs. It was not her plan but she couldn't help herself.

'Madam?' the girl called after her. 'Your brochure?'

The stairs were carpeted in a migraine-inducing pattern; abstract prints hung up the walls. Rose reached the first floor as the lift wheezed open and P stepped out and turned towards Room 12. Rose watched. She watched the swing of P's hips inside her coat, she watched her pause outside the door, take out a lipstick, wind it up, press it to her lips and blot them with a tissue. She watched her lick a finger and slick each eyebrow. She watched her pat her hair before she knocked. She watched the door open and swallow the woman. And then she stood and watched the door, for twenty minutes or so. It was a perfectly ordinary door with a brass number 12 and a spyhole like a fish's eye, but only for looking out of. If she could have peered in, would she? She caught a movement and jumped at the pallid blur of her own reflection, in the glass over an abstract nightmare in black and red.

After a time she took the lift down; the interior smelled, she thought, faintly of that furry musk, a crushed and vaguely meaty smell.

'Watch me do anything,' he'd said.

Hair dry enough now, she brushes it, enjoying the painful snarl of tangles. She rubs in the rose body cream he's bought her every year since their first Christmas. She unfolds a fresh nightie enjoying the smooth, ironed cotton falling over her skin. Eyes might dim and hearing fade, sense of taste become less acute but the sense of touch, that doesn't go.

Her bare soles pick up grit from the landing carpet. Tomorrow she'll get out the vacuum, have a proper go at it. How hard to stay clean for even a moment in this world.

Eric's asleep, his mouth hanging open, trailing drool. She eases the book from his hand, picks up the postcard he uses as a bookmark. It's a view of Venice, sent by Gina many years ago.

Dear Mum and Dad, I know how you love the city, and so do I. Though it's a bit smelly isn't it? Went all down the Grand Canal in a Gondola. Love you, Gina.

Rose puts it in the book and closes it. Gently she removes Eric's specs, putting them on top of the book ready for him to reach for in the morning.

She bends down to look more closely at his face, bleached to a weird radiance by his special daylight lamp. You can see the ghost of the sexy man – sexy man she managed to keep despite it all. After he'd dropped P there'd been no one much; no one serious, and he'd been flattened, quieter, *tireder*. But he'd been there.

She examines the line of the nose, the shape of lips, thin now, liverish and wet. Behind them the teeth are grey. No one would want to kiss those lips now, no other woman. The breath that struggles out between them has a smell she does not want to recognise. The whole room has taken on that smell.

She goes to the window and draws back the curtain to allow in the freshness of a summer night. Light from the room slants down onto the daisy-spattered lawn: all those tiny pursed up petals glowing.

Watch me do anything, he said. He hasn't many weeks to go, the doctor tells her. And she will be here, watching.

GUY WARE

HOSTAGE

I knew you once: but in Paradise,
If we meet, I will pass nor turn my face.
– Browning

1

All the way home she had the feeling something wasn't right. It was late, but not too late for the last train, and dark on the walk from the station – but what would she expect? Autumn had almost collapsed into winter: the last leaves huddled around streetlights like pickets at a brazier, throwing the pavements into irregular, shifting shadow. She was drunk, of course, but that wasn't it. Outside the station the road works that had been there in the morning, that had been there for weeks, weren't there. The corner shop was closed, its windows shuttered and blank. It was after midnight . . . of course it was shut. She was just drunk.

The team had been out after work, because it was Thursday and the markets had been up and down, but mostly because it was Thursday. She and Shazia had downed a couple of margaritas before someone started in on pitchers of sangria. When the lights came on – bright, scouring lights that showed up all your pores – the bouncers held the doors open, letting cold November air do their work for them. They said, Haven't you got homes to go to? Yes, she thought, she had.

So: she was drunk – drunker than she probably ought to be at her age, on a Thursday; drunk enough to fall asleep on the train. Ordinary drunk, then – not paralytic, not like she couldn't walk; and anyway, it wasn't that. It was just something floating in the corner of her eye. Something tugging at her like a detail in a thriller she knew must be a clue if she could only work out why. Sometimes, she'd try to puzzle them out, but mostly she would just plough on, knowing it made no difference, knowing it would work itself out anyway.

The back door was unlocked, the way he left it when she was out late. She dropped her case in the kitchen, by the table; in the dark she could just make out a small pile of keys, a mobile and a couple of letters, one from the bank.

She climbed the stairs. Rob had rolled over to her side of the bed. She tipped him back as far as she dared and slipped in beside him. He rolled again and curled his arm around her, kissed the back of her neck, but she knew he was still asleep. She peeled him off and shoved him onto his back, hoping he wouldn't snore.

When she woke, his side of the bed was warm, but he wasn't there. Then he *was* there, at the window, cracking open the blinds on a drear, grey winter's morning, saying brightly: 'Another day in paradise.'

She curled herself tighter and pulled the sheet over her head. He said, 'Don't let your coffee get cold. Love you.' Then he left.

She thought she heard other voices – high, light, insubstantial – before the front door closed and a car engine coughed into life outside. She pushed back the sheet. She must be late. The grey November light was bright enough to pin shut her eyes. She opened them again more slowly.

The blond IKEA wardrobe with the loose hinge was on the wrong side of the room. It should have been on the left, in the alcove between the fireplace and the bay window instead of on the right. She got out of bed, supporting her head with her hands, and opened the wardrobe door. The clothes were not hers. They were *like* hers: the labels and the styles seemed familiar, but familiar like memories, not like daily life. The shoes were mostly flats and there was no sign of the silk and mohair suit she usually wore to shore up a hangover. She picked something equally expensive but functional, and headed downstairs to the kitchen, where she found a table with three dirty bowls and glasses and, clasped to the fridge by a hinged magnetic frog, a photograph of a man being hugged by two identical girls, all tangles of dark shiny hair blown across perfect adolescent skin, upon whom she knew, with a sudden, cold-eyed sobriety beyond all doubt, she had never in her life set eyes before.

2

He had read, or heard – he could not now be sure which, or when; but the dictum had stuck in his head because it had seemed so extravagantly untrue – that all relationships are power relationships, that one partner always holds more power than the other, and that the power depends on the weakness of the other, on which of them needs the other more; no equilibrium is ever reached.

A few years later, it had seemed to him true; it seemed to him, furthermore, that *he* had the power; that, of the two of them, it was she who needed him, he who could, if it came to it, just walk away.

Then they had the girls – twins – and everything became harder. Harder to stay; harder even to imagine leaving, until one day – the girls would have been nine – he had watched

Aimee screw up her eyes and push the plunger on the hypodermic in her diabetic mother's thigh while Nicole looked on, her face a perfect blend of fascination and disgust, and he realised quite suddenly, without having thought of it for years, that he no longer had the power, that the woman he thought he had chosen to love had acquired reinforcements. It was now unthinkable for him to live without her strength, much less abandon it of his own accord. And then she disappeared.

3

Shazia, pressing her hand over the mouthpiece of her telephone, said: 'You're late.'

'It's a long story.'

Shazia grinned. 'I saw the first four acts.' She widened her eyes, expecting gossip. But, as Ines dumped her bag and slumped into her chair, a tropical-grade shit-storm broke over the world of traded reinsurance and for the next seven hours neither she nor Shazia had time to talk. A tidal wave of greed and fear rushed west towards them, gathering pace as one by one the eastern markets closed, until the wave broke, somewhere over Amsterdam and they were done and could leave the Yanks to wipe up the mess. They reckoned they were maybe just the tiniest fraction of a point ahead. But at least they hadn't lost, and it was the weekend.

They were waiting for four Bloody Marys – it saved time queuing – when Shazia demanded details. 'You weren't sick on the tube?'

Ines told her some of it, while Shazia listened, open-mouthed. 'This happened? This isn't something you daydreamed on the way in?'

Ines shook her head.

'Really?'

'Really.' Ines paid for the drinks and they shoved their way to a corner where there was a shelf large enough to put their glasses down.

'You must have realised? I mean, come on.'

Ines thought about the picture of the man with the two girls. But she wasn't going to mention that, not even to Shazia. Instead she said that as she left the house that morning – a between-the-wars semi like her own, but with a gate on the right hand side of the garden, not the left – as soon as she began walking to the tube, it was obvious what had happened. She'd just turned the wrong way.

Shazia said, 'Well that explains everything.'

'Last night. At Bank, you know?' Ines said. 'Where you go down the escalator, and then back on yourself and down again, and then turn right for northbound and left for south, or whichever way it is. I do it every day and I still couldn't say for sure. I just don't look. But, whatever, I must have turned the wrong way. By the time I got to the station this morning I was sure it was going to be Morden, Collier's Wood, something like that.'

'And was it?'

'South Wimbledon.'

'Class.' Shazia lived in Clerkenwell; Ines somewhere further north than Shazia said she'd ever been, somewhere just below the M25.

They finished their first drinks, started the second. When it looked like Ines wasn't going to say anything more, Shazia said, 'Was he cute?'

Ines honestly didn't know: she hadn't looked.

'So he could be?'

'That's not the point.'

'It's always the point. If he's cute, you could have this whole secret life thing going on. How exciting is that? You could just disappear into the fantasy world of . . . South Wimbledon.'

Shazia's straight face cracked. Choking on laughter and vodka she pointed at Ines: 'Your face!'

'I don't want to disappear. I don't want a new start. That's what men do.'

Shazia sighed. 'Men, right.'

'Right. Men rip everything up and start again when they can't cope with what they've got.' Then she thought of the photo on the fridge, of the man and the two girls, arms around each other, smiling, eyes screwed up against the sunshine.

'So what did you tell Rob?'

'I crashed at your place?'

Shazia shook her head, but it was mock disbelief, not refusal.

Ines thought she was the best. An angel.

Shazia said, 'And tonight?'

'Tonight?'

'What are you going to do?'

Ines looked at her friend, whose face was not quite in focus.

'At Bank. Tonight. Are you turning left or right?'

4

It had been a good week. Grief had kept its distance, slinking like a cowed dog in the shadows, never coming up too close. The twins hadn't mentioned their mother; there'd been no junk mail in her name. But this afternoon he'd left work early, knowing what would happen. The bank had written to them both: their fixed-rate mortgage deal – the deal she had arranged – was about to expire; if they did nothing the monthly payments would go up a hundred pounds or so. Another hundred pounds he didn't have, on top of all the other hundreds of pounds he didn't have now she wasn't here, wasn't working, wasn't being paid.

In the bank he sat at a wooden table in a frosted glass box

while an adviser showed him leaflets, scribbling rings around figures with a ball-point pen. She said they could save him money, then gave him the forms and said to bring them in when he and his wife had both signed. And there it was, the black dog, snarling, saliva dripping from its teeth.

'I've been through this.'

'I'm sorry?'

'I've been through this with you – with this bank – a hundred times.'

'I don't understand, Mr Bridges. It's a joint mortgage; we need both your signatures.'

He found himself goading the dog on. 'I wish to God I could get my wife to sign the forms, but I can't. I can't.'

'I don't understand.'

'Watch my lips. I don't. Have. A wife.'

She said, 'I'm very sorry, Mr Bridges. If . . . there's been . . . some change in your circumstances . . . '

And he was off, roaring, now. 'Change? That's the problem, isn't it? Nothing changes. Five years. Five *years*. You know this. I'm not divorced. She's not dead. She's missing. If she were dead the insurance would pay the whole fucking mortgage and I wouldn't have to be here!'

The door to the glass box opened. Two men in suits stood in the corridor. The older one said, 'Is everything all right, Alice?'

He'd done what he could. He'd reported her disappearance to the police. She'd gone to work, he said. She'd left her phone, her keys and her insulin on the kitchen table, and just not come back. The policewoman made notes, and he said forgetting stuff wasn't that unusual. It wasn't the point. She had spare medicine at work. But no one had seen her since Thursday morning. The policewoman told him not to worry. Lots of people go missing: three quarters turn up within forty-eight hours. But it was already Saturday. He hadn't reported it on Friday because he thought she might have gone out after work and stayed over with a friend. She did that sometimes. The policewoman said ninety-nine percent turned up within a year. A year? A *year*? He'd thought she was going to say a week or two.

Later, when a year had passed and he'd put up posters and trawled the internet and a friend had made him a website so people could report they'd seen her; when he'd followed up the first few sightings and been to Hove and Middlesbrough and Cardiff with photos in his hand, and had caught himself about to buy a ticket to Denver, Colorado; when he'd had a serious conversation with someone at the support group about visiting a medium, even though he'd never, ever believed in all that crap; when, after all that, he read on one of the sites he still looked at that 210,000 people are reported missing in England and Wales every year, and he calculated that, even if ninety-nine percent turned up – one way or another, because he knew by now they didn't all turn up alive, or happy to be found – setting that aside, he worked out, even one percent still meant that more than two thousand people simply vanished – for ever – each and every year: about six a day, every day.

Had he done everything he could? Of course he hadn't. And if he had, what difference would it make?

Just a week ago, Aimee had said it would be her friend Rosie's birthday at the weekend and she was going to sleep over at Rosie's house, OK? And he had said it wasn't. It was not OK. He said you had to plan these things, you couldn't just up and disappear without talking to people first. Aimee said she *was* talking to him. She said: 'No wonder Mum walked out!' He knew it was a teenage ritual, but he still felt sick, winded. He felt as if he'd never breathe again. He felt the way he'd felt when Aimee, as a toddler, had waddled between parked cars out into the road and he'd watched, paralysed, as a taxi driver slammed his brakes and swerved and the wheels of his monstrous cab rolled over her feet. He shouted, at the toddler, at the teenager. He howled and raged and part of him watched, a small voice in the back of his head saying, *Is that the best that you can do?*

5

It took seven years, but when the sonographer somehow plucked twins from the blizzard of their early scans they were as happy and scared and excited as any parents could be. When it became clear that the twins were conjoined, they listened to the doctors and they read reports Rob printed off the internet and they knew that they would cope. They read about Chang and Eng Bunker, the 'Siamese Twins' who travelled with PT Barnum's Circus; about the Chalkhurst sisters, Mary and Elizabeth, born in Kent in the twelfth century and still commemorated in local cakes. They read about separation techniques and survival rates. The next time they saw the consultant he told them that, in a small number of cases – less than ten percent – one of the conjoined twins was smaller, less developed and parasitic on its larger sibling.

Ines said, 'Parasitic?'

'It will never mature and cannot survive independently.'

Rob said, '*She*.'

They agreed, just before the birth, that they had no choice. The parasitic twin would die, the doctors could say that at least. But about her host – her *sister*, Rob said – they were less secure: her life was bracketed around with percentages.

Rob said the percentages made no difference, and she agreed. Now that they had come this far, there was no choice.

6

When he got back from the bank he found a letter for Mrs Bridges – she rarely used her married name – from a catalogue company; on his laptop was an email from a man who'd seen her in Coalville, which turned out to be in Leicestershire. He opened the letter in case she'd made a purchase that might give him some kind of clue, at least tell him she had been alive.

It was a random mail-shot.

Nicole came into the kitchen. She stood behind his chair, laid her chin on his shoulder. She said she'd finished her homework, would he like her to cook dinner? He asked where Aimee was.

'Drum class, Dad. It's Thursday.'

Aimee came home just before six, and he caught a look between the girls that said what kind of day he'd had. She said, 'Hi, Dad. You're home early.'

Nicole said, 'He went to the bank.'

'And?'

Nicole shook her head.

Aimee said, 'Shit.'

He looked up, let it go.

Sometimes, she came back. He'd leave the door unlocked and sometimes, like tonight, when the girls were asleep and the house was quiet, he'd pour himself a whisky – even though he had work tomorrow – and take the tumbler and the bottle up to her study in the attic and scour the internet for signs, for any faint electromagnetic trace she might have left to prove she was alive. Or dead. No longer knowing which he wanted most. It was on nights like these that he would creep downstairs to bed at two or three a.m., and she would come home, late from some work do, and slip silently into bed beside him; he would wrap an arm around her waist and kiss the back of her neck. She would not be there in the morning. Sometimes he wondered what he would do if she ever were.

He put the letter back in its envelope. The gummed strip was sticky enough to re-seal. He turned it over, crossed out her name and wrote: *Not known at this address.*

7

That night, at Bank, she hugged and kissed Shazia goodbye. She took the escalator down, then down again. At the bottom, she turned left, or right – whichever – and caught the train that came. She would plough on, knowing it would make no difference now that she had come this far, knowing it would work itself out anyway.

MJ HYLAND

EVEN PRETTY EYES COMMIT CRIMES

I'D WALKED HOME after a twelve-hour nightshift to save on bus fares, and to clear my head, and by the time I got to my flat, I was desperate for a shower and some kip.

But there'd be no sleeping that morning: when I turned the corner, there was my father, sitting on my doorstep and holding a pineapple.

He hadn't told me he was coming and I'd no idea what he was doing there. We hadn't seen each other for a few months, mostly because I'd stopped inviting him round. Things weren't good between me and my wife and I didn't want him to know about our troubles.

'Hello, Dad.'

'Ah, there you are, James.'

'What are you doing here so early?'

'It's after eight o'clock. I was about to head off. I thought you'd be home earlier.'

My father didn't wear a watch but seemed always to know the time.

'I had to stay on a bit longer,' I said. 'The ward was short-staffed and ten hours turned into twelve.'

Besides the pineapple he had nothing else with him, not

even his briefcase, which he took everywhere. He was dressed like a tourist; crisp, clean khaki shorts, long white socks and a short-sleeved shirt. 'I was hoping to chat with you for a minute,' he said. 'If that's alright.'

Chatting on the doorstep was the last thing I wanted. Not with the sun boring a hole in the back of my neck.

'OK,' I said. 'But I'll be hitting the sack soon.'

'I won't keep you long, son. You must be knackered.'

He was right, but he didn't know the half of it.

'Yes, I am,' I said. 'I've been on the graveyards for six weeks.'

'Graveyard shifts! I bet there aren't many in St Vincent's who like you saying that.'

'Dead right,' I said.

He smiled, and I did too.

The next-door neighbours' dogs started barking then, loud and sharp. They were old dogs, kept tied to a concrete post with short ropes, and when the day was gearing up to be a scorcher, they seemed to sense they'd soon run out of water, and then the barking started, panicked and piercing.

My father shook his head.

'Those Italians need to train their Kelpies to stop barking,' he said.

'Or look after them better.'

'You should call the RSPCA.'

'I will. You're right.'

He shook his head. 'Poor sods.'

I was desperate to go inside, rest my legs and get rid of my hot shoes and socks.

'So, do you want to come in?'

'If it's not too much trouble.'

'We'd best be quiet, though,' I said. 'Janice won't be out of bed yet.'

I held out my hand – to help him up from the doorstep.

'Here, Dad. Grab hold.'

'I'm alright,' he said. 'No need.'

I'd had thirty years to get used to Australian summers, long days with no distinct parts – hot in the morning, noon and night – with a glare that came off every footpath and parked car; a heat so strong it'd killed dozens of people; mostly pale Brits and the like, who went outback in brand-new caravans, all done up with extra cupboards and foldaway-beds, and never came out again.

My father, on the other hand, was made better by the sun; it made him even more buoyant. He might've been sixty-five, but on that morning, I was more beaten and tired than he'd ever been.

'Where's your car?'

'At the mechanics.'

I hadn't noticed my car was gone but it wasn't at the mechanics, and that meant my wife had taken it, and she didn't like to drive; not unless she had a load of shopping and needed the boot or she had some passengers.

'Let's get inside,' I said.

My father went in ahead of me and while I took off my shoes, he stood in the hallway and took a long, hard look round.

He peered through the opened doors into the lounge-room, kitchen and bedroom and this wasn't idle prying: he was looking for Janice, and he was looking for her because he suspected her of straying, the same way he'd suspected my mother.

'Where's Janice?' he said. 'She works in the afternoons, doesn't she?'

'She's probably gone to the shops.'

She hadn't gone to the shops and it was obvious the bed hadn't been slept in, and wherever she was, she must've taken off during the night, probably not long after our fight over money and after she said this as I was heading out the door for work:

'You're boring now, James.'

So, maybe it was over. The way she'd said this had a cool and expert tone, a bit like my mother's tone when she analysed people, mostly people she didn't like, or couples who sit in cafés reading the newspaper and not talking to each other. 'They're boring each other,' my mother used to say. 'They're probably only days away from divorce.'

While I changed into a pair of sandals, my father looked at the wedding photos on the wall above the phone table.

'I had more hair then, didn't I?'

'Yes, and I was a bit taller.'

I'm not sure why I said this, except maybe that when I looked at the photographs of me and Janice – taken two years ago – both of us all done up in our finery, I looked happy, probably happier than I really was. That's the problem with photographs.

'The shops don't open till nine,' he said. 'Maybe she's gone to that Jewish deli. The one down on Florence Street. They even make bagels on Christmas Day.'

'I don't know, Dad. But it doesn't really matter. She'll be back soon enough.'

I'd no idea where she'd gone, and if she was gone for good this time, and my father was going to see the very thing he'd predicted the last time he'd come round to the flat. Janice had gone off to stay with her sister for a few days and my father said, 'I hope you don't mind me saying, but Janice even looks a bit like your mother. Don't you think? And she's . . . what? Seven years younger than you? Not far off the difference between me and your mother . . .' and on he went.

We went into the kitchen, which was sticky with a humid, wet heat. I opened the window over the sink to let some air flow through and had a look into the yard – or the concrete patch – which we shared with ten other tenants.

The cat from No.12 was sleeping, curled up on the trampoline, and Janice's bike was gone. Had she stuck it in the boot of the car, or strapped it to the roof-rack, and if she had, who the hell was helping her?

My father sat at the table and held the pineapple in his lap.

'Will you be wanting to change out of your uniform and put it in the wash?'

He was more like a woman with all his fussing.

'No need, Dad. I've got plenty more.'

'It's fine weather,' he said. 'Another beautiful day.'

'Too right,' I said. 'If you like being in an oven.'

'Here,' he said, 'this pineapple's yours. What a glorious country, eh? Fresh tropical fruit all year round.'

'I don't really like pineapples, Dad. Why don't you give it to somebody at the surgery?'

'Well, it won't go to waste, that's for sure.'

'No. I'm sure you'll find somebody to adopt it. Maybe take it to the pound. There aren't many pineapples with such a happy wagging tail as that fine specimen.'

He laughed. 'You forgot to mention that it won't go pining for long. Get it?'

I smiled, as real a smile as I could manage.

'Yes, I get it.'

'But seriously, son. You should eat more fruit.'

'I know.'

I wanted to sit, but I was so anxious my whole body vibrated and I didn't want him to see me like this. And if I sat down, he'd stay longer.

'What do you want to drink, Dad? Will a cup of tea do?'

'That'd hit the spot nicely.'

There was no milk in the fridge.

'Sorry, Dad. There's only powdered milk.'

'Then I'll have water,' he said. 'Do you have ice?'

There was no ice in the freezer, but I went ahead and rummaged and the frost took some of the heat off my hands. I was burning up.

'There's no ice,' I said.

'Forget the water, then. I'll suck on one of these.'

He took a packet of Fisherman's Friends from the back pocket of his khaki shorts.

'Do you want one?'

'No, thanks. They make me cough.'

He got up from the table and I thought he was going to leave. I didn't want him to stay and I didn't want him to see me sweating, and yet, I didn't want to be alone either.

But he didn't leave: he went to the sink and put the pineapple on the draining board, tried to stand it upright, and when it toppled, he held its bottom and moved it round 'til he was sure it wouldn't budge.

'What time do you start work?'

'There's no mad rush, son. I've arranged for the locum to get things started.'

'Thanks for the pineapple,' I said. 'Janice will love it.'

'Is she still selling buttons?'

'No, she . . . it wasn't buttons, it's a storage warehouse . . .'

I'd nearly let it slip that she'd been sacked.

'I was only kidding, son. I know what she does.'

He went off to the loo, and as soon as he'd closed the door, he turned the portable radio on. He didn't like the sound of a flushing toilet, which was a strange and squeamish thing for a doctor. Even the sound of somebody eating made him feel – what did he say? – '. . . a bit embarrassed'.

As usual, he was in the bathroom a long time, even after he'd flushed, he stayed a while, and he was probably spraying air freshener.

While he was busy in the loo, I had time to check both my mobile and the landline. There was nothing from Janice, no message, not even a bitter or angry one. Nothing.

Then, the bedroom: Janice had cleared out most of her clothes, even the clothes in the laundry hamper, and there'd be no point checking the bedside drawers: I knew they'd be empty too. Though she'd threatened leaving a couple of times, I didn't believe she would, not so suddenly: people didn't end marriages without warning, without a second chance. But after the fight last night, and what she said about me being boring, I suppose I should've known this time was different.

When my father came back into the kitchen he smelt of Brut and this meant he'd been in the bathroom cupboards, and he'd probably seen that none of her stuff was there.

And so, I'd no choice but to sit at the table and wait for him to say what he'd come to say. But he said nothing and we faced each other, neither of us speaking – not a word.

'So, how've you been?' he said. 'How are you keeping?'

'Not too bad. The graveyards are hard, but I like the quiet hours when the patients are sleeping. And the walk home is good.'

More silence.

'Is that broken?'

He was talking about the ceiling fan.

'Yes. The landlord's going to send somebody to fix it.'

He looked into the yard.

'Didn't Janice leave you a note or anything?'

'Jesus Christ, Dad. I'm not her minder and she's not my bloody secretary. Give it a rest, won't you.'

'Just wondering is all,' he said. 'No need to bite my head off.'

When I was fifteen, my mother ran away, packed her case and disappeared. I knew she wasn't happy – I'd heard a lot of their fights late at night – but I didn't think she'd leave, not in a million years, and I didn't know she'd left until I came home from school and my father came to my bedroom, and sat on the end of my bed.

'This is going to come as a big shock, son, but I've got some bad news.'

Maybe I'd been expelled from school, which would've made it a second time, but when I saw my father's neck turn red, I knew it was much worse.

'Your mother's left us, and she won't be coming back.'

'Why?'

'Just listen for a minute. Can you do that?'

I nodded.

'She's gone to London. She needs to be with your granny, who's very sick, as you know.'

'Why couldn't we go with her?'

'That wouldn't be possible now, would it?'

'Why not? Why couldn't I go?'

'Because she'll be living with your granny in a one-bed maisonette in Tottenham Court Road, and you need to finish school, that's why.'

'Why didn't she say goodbye?'

'She was too upset. And she didn't have much time.'

He stopped talking then and looked confused, as though he hadn't expected questions, or didn't know how to tell the story.

'Your granny has taken a very bad turn and she hasn't got long left. Your mother needs to be with her.'

'So, she'll come back then? After Granny's died?'

'No, James. That's the thing. Your mother has made the difficult decision that she can't live in Australia any more. Her nose bleeds, as you know, and she's allergic to the heat and she has those cramps . . . '

'She didn't tell me. Why didn't she tell me?'

'Listen, son. I know you're hurting. I'm hurting too.'

'Yeah?' I said. 'Doesn't bloody look like it.'

He stared at me the same way he sometimes stared at her; as though he didn't know who I was.

'Well,' he said, 'maybe we should talk in the morning. Get some sleep. Alright?'

My father made himself some dinner that night and ate alone in his study – the room he called his 'den' and which, with a camper bed and a small bedside table, soon became his bedroom. A few hours later he came back to my bedroom and, like before, sat on the end of my bed.

'She didn't leave because she doesn't love you,' he said. 'She left because she felt she had no choice.'

He put his hand on my knee.

'I'm not an idiot, Dad. You must've got rid of her. And I'm leaving. And you have to pay for my ticket and everything.'

'You can't leave in your final year of school.'

'Then I'll go when I've finished school.'

'Let's not make any rash decisions.'

'You're lying,' I said. 'Leave me alone.'

As he left my room, he turned off the light, and he also switched off the light in the hallway.

'Turn the hall light back on,' I shouted.

He came back and stood at the end of my bed, his arms folded.

'You're nearly sixteen, James, and you're still afraid of the dark. She's made you too soft. Maybe some time apart will be good for you.'

'How would you know what I'm afraid of? And so what if I am?'

He tried to smile.

'You're right, son. We all have our peculiarities. I shouldn't have said that.'

'You made her leave, didn't you?'

'Please don't do this, son. I'm very sorry she's left us and it's not my fault.'

'Leave me alone. I'm going to sleep. And don't close the bloody door.'

He looked at me, but with a softer face.

'If you plan on taking this out on me, I hope you'll reconsider. We need to get through this together. The alternative is disastrous.'

I felt like spewing and I had a nervous gut that felt almost the same as bad hunger, after a whole day without food. I wanted him to stay with me and I wanted to make peace with him but I went on accusing him and it wasn't the last time I crucified and punished him when I'd stopped being angry and wanted to be nice with him.

About a year into our marriage, when Janice and I started to argue, mostly about petty things – like her habit of going to the shops to buy cigarettes and not telling me she was going, and not asking me if I needed anything – instead of letting it drop, I'd go at her, and made the sour mood worse, and even when she'd said sorry, and I wasn't angry any more, I held to the anger, and it was never about the thing that had started it off.

Though it was only nine o'clock, the kitchen was stifling hot and the backs of my knees were sticky with sweat.

'So, Dad. You said you wanted to talk about something.'

I straightened my shoulders, tried to give myself a bit more height, to hide my worry and fatigue.

'Yes. I've been meaning to ask you whether you've given any more thought to taking the exam.'

He meant the mature-age medical school exam and he'd asked me about it the last time he came round, and the time before that.

'Not yet.' I said. 'I'm not sure.'

'Do you think you'll work as a nurse for the rest of your life?'

'I might, Dad. I like it. Plenty of people do. It's weird that nobody seems to know the stats. All the research shows that people in lowly jobs are often happier than high-flyers. How come that's so hard to believe?'

'Alright. OK. Let's drop it. But, what about –'

'Dad, stop it. *Please.*'

But the way I must've looked to him that morning was more proof to him that I needed a better job, a better life.

'How's your blood pressure been of late?'

'Normal, Dad. It's normal.'

'Do you still get those dizzy spells? Maybe while I'm here I could check your vitals?'

'I can check my own bloody pulse. There's no need.'

'You look a bit flushed. A bit iffy around the gills.'

'There's nothing wrong with me. It's just stuffy in here. I feel like I'm wearing a bear suit.'

'I see,' he said. 'You never did warm to the heat.'

He laughed at his own joke, a right schoolboy.

'Good one,' I said. 'That's a good one.'

We both tried to smile, and then, more silence.

The only sound came from the traffic in Ormond Road – the delivery trucks beeping as they reversed out of the Mornflake warehouse.

He wasn't troubled by the silence, or the lack of something

to do with his hands. He was tidy and ambitious and he liked his own company and even a stranger could see it; the way he sat with his hands on the knees of his khaki shorts, the creases just as they were when he pulled them, brand new, from the box.

After my mother left, my father and I lived together for five years and, for most of those years, when he got home from the surgery, I'd be stuck with him, trapped in the kitchen or lounge-room, with all his talking, his always-right views on life, and when I went into my bedroom, and he wanted to check on my homework, he'd just barge in, and I'd have to yawn my head right off its hinges to get rid of him.

Most weekends I'd pretend to be going into the city to see a film with friends and instead I'd catch the bus to an internet café three suburbs away and drink Coke and play games online and I sometimes tried to find my mother.

When I was in my second year at uni, he asked me to have a drink with him.

'It's time we had a proper man-to-man chat,' he said. 'Make sure you can spare me at least an hour or so.'

We met on a perfect spring day, a gentle day, and we sat in the corner of a dark pub, near a television perched on beer kegs.

After a bit of small-talk, he said, 'It's time I told you a few home-truths. About your mother.'

'OK,' I said. 'Go ahead.'

'Well, for starters, I knew your mother was up to no good years before she left us.'

As far as I was concerned, she hadn't left *us* – she'd left *him*. She'd got sick of him and found somebody else. I was only fifteen, but I wasn't stupid. I'd heard her yelling at him, and I'd heard her say 'Men shouldn't talk as much as you do, Richard' and I'd heard her accuse him of killing the cat.

My father sipped his beer slowly and looked at the TV for a while. There was a cricket match on, which he loved, and I didn't.

'She was a very good actress, your mother,' he said. 'A very good liar.'

I was too angry to speak. What he'd said got me in the gut, a weird kind of wetness low in my stomach and when he came back to the table after ordering another round, he put the drinks down and sat closer and, after a moment, as though he was a different person, he put his hand on my knee.

'I'll tell you something now,' he said. 'Even pretty eyes commit crimes. You should bear that in mind when you start making lady friends.'

'Right,' I said.

'You prefer ladies, don't you?'

'Of course I do,' I said. 'Jesus Christ!'

I moved my leg.

'Well then,' he said. 'You've been warned. You thought your mother was an angel because she looked like one, but you were completely wrong about that.'

'Right,' I said. 'So she didn't go home to England to look after Granny.'

'No.'

'I'm going to the loo,' I said.

I'd had enough of him. I took the long way round to the door, past the toilets, and behind the dining area.

'Where are you going?' he said.

He'd followed me, was standing right behind me as I tugged at the door.

'Sorry, Dad. I need to go back to uni. I have to meet my tutor.'

He followed me out to the street. 'Did you hear what I said before? Were you listening?'

'Yes, but I have to go to a lecture.'

'You need to wake up to the facts,' he said. 'Do you follow me?'

'Yes,' I said.

The bus stop was a few feet away and a bus was pulling in.

'I have to go,' I said.

'James,' he said. 'Wait a minute.'

I turned back.

'I've made things worse, haven't I?'

He moved to me and I suppose he wanted to give me a fatherly pat, maybe a hug, and he never found that kind of thing easy, neither of us did.

'Wait a minute, James. Just hear me out.'

The bus was gone.

'I know I've made things worse. I shouldn't have told you the truth. I only want the best for you.'

Though I wanted the same as he did – no more being at war, some affection – I was too hurt, too angry, and all I did was shrug.

'Whatever you say, Dad.'

'Are you alright?' he said.

'Yeah. Alright,' I said.

'You missed your bus. Here . . . '

He took a few notes from his wallet.

'Catch a taxi. I don't want you to be late.'

'No need,' I said. 'I'll walk.'

We saw very little of each other after that spring afternoon; maybe once or twice a year, my birthday and Christmas, but that changed when I married Janice.

On our wedding day, at a small outdoor gathering by the

lake, he gave me our wedding gift, which had been wrapped by his favourite department store, David Jones. He gave us a tartan picnic flask, a picnic basket with six matching cups and plates, and a tartan rug. 'You'll have a family of your own, soon,' he said. 'And I want to help you along. I can help you get on with things. I can help you sort things out.'

And here he was at the flat again, another visit, and I think he probably knew how bad things had become.

There was no air whatsoever coming through the kitchen window, so I opened the back door and, soon as it was open, the cat jumped off the trampoline and came inside, came right in, sniffed at the cupboard under the sink, and looked at us, then sat, as though waiting for something.

'Is that your cat?' he said.

'No. It belongs to the upstairs neighbour.'

'Why does it come in here?'

'That's what cats do.'

'It stinks,' he said. 'Is it neutered? You should tell them upstairs that neutering is a relatively cheap and simple operation.'

'I will.'

We both looked at the cat, which was panting from the heat.

'How about you, Dad? How've you been?'

'I could use a bit more help,' he said. 'My secretary's always behind. Things are getting to be too much for us. I've been wondering if I should retire.'

'Maybe you need a new secretary, then.'

'Don't be daft, son. I've spent too long training her. Anyway, the patients are very fond of her. She keeps teddy bears behind the desk for the kiddies.'

'That's good then, Dad,' I said. 'If the patients like her, isn't that more important than paperwork?'

'You're right, son. Of course, you're right.'

~

The baby in the flat upstairs started howling. I'd had enough.

'Listen, Dad. I might have a bit of a sleep now, if that's alright.'

'Won't you be waking up again soon?' he said. 'When Janice gets home?'

'That's not a problem. I'll go straight back to sleep.'

He stood.

'I'll get out of your hair then, will I?'

We faced each other across the table, and he looked at me, and we were breathing in unison. I'd hardly ever seen the look he had in his eyes that morning, as though he was trying to memorise my face, or seeing it for the first time.

And he didn't want to leave.

'Listen, Dad. Stay for a bit,' I said. 'I can sleep later.'

'Alright, son. I'll stay for a bit.'

'But go into the lounge-room. It's a bit cooler in there.

I told him to go in ahead of me, that I needed to use the loo and freshen up. I put my head under the cold tap, drenched myself then dried off, and I changed my shirt and got two glasses of orange juice.

Before I went into the lounge-room, I stopped in the hallway to take a breath and from just outside the door I saw my father. He was looking out the window and couldn't see me and he'd unclenched his jaw, let his mouth hang open and I saw the way he looked in repose, when nobody else was around and he didn't have his face ready; not strong, and not so sure of himself.

He looked like an older man and I was sure he was thinking about my mother. I sensed it in his face, his slackened mouth and, for a moment, I thought of her, too, and it was the memory that always came first, though I didn't want it.

~

A few months before my mother left home, it was a winter's day, and the three of us were eating lunch in her favourite café. She told the waitress she wanted something that wasn't on the menu: 'A large onion sandwich.'

The waitress was still at our table and my father laughed. 'Precisely how large is a large onion?' he said.

When the waitress left, my mother stood up.

'The waitress knew what I meant,' she said. 'Everybody else knew what I meant, Richard. What the hell's wrong with you?'

My father tried to apologise.

'Oh, pet,' he said. 'Don't feel that way.'

Her coat was hanging on the back of my father's chair and she needed him to sit forward to get it.

'Move!' she said.

He turned round to her, put his hand on her arm, and tried to console her as best he could – as he often did – by holding onto a part of her.

'I said move!' she said. 'You slow, deaf old pig! I need my coat.'

But my father didn't move quickly enough and she wrenched the coat from behind his back.

'You're embarrassing me, Richard,' she said. 'Get off my bloody coat!'

I moved into the lounge-room.

'Sorry I took so long, Dad.'

'I've opened the window and turned on the fan for you,' he said.

'Thanks. Here's some OJ.'

I sat on the end of the settee and he sat in the armchair nearest the door. As we sat, we crossed our legs, left over right, a genetic tic, something the both of us did whenever we sat.

'I think I'll call Janice,' I said. 'I'll ask her to bring some milk and ice back with her.'

The phone was warm in my hand and he waited for me to check for messages.

But still there were none. Nothing.

'She's on her way home,' I said.

'Alright,' he said. 'I should be heading off soon anyway.'

But he was going to stay. He was going to wait with me until she came home – or didn't.

We were silent for a while and we watched a Mornflake truck reversing out of the warehouse and then my father scratched his arm.

'There might be fleas in here,' he said, 'from that cat. Have you been bitten?'

'No. I haven't. It was probably a mozzie.'

'What's that white stuff in the carpet,' he said. 'Those little flecks . . . I thought it might be flea powder.'

'No, it's sand,' I said. 'It's hard to get rid of.'

'Never mind,' he said. 'A small price to pay for such a nice location.'

We lived less than ten minutes from Bondi Beach and that was part of the reason why we paid so much rent for such a cramped and gloomy flat.

I wanted to move out to the suburbs – just for a few years – to save some money for an air-conditioner, and maybe a trip to Europe, but Janice refused. She said she couldn't stand the stench of the suburban sticks and so we stayed in our sweat-box, which we couldn't afford, and bought three fans; four fans, including the busted ceiling fan in the kitchen.

I looked at my father and swirled the orange juice round as though the glass had ice in it.

'You can check your mobile phone again if you want,' he said. 'You look a bit worried, or something.'

'I'm not worried, Dad. She'll be here in a minute. And then we'll have ice and milk, and then I'm going to hit the sack.'

He stood, and it seemed abrupt, sudden, as though he'd heard a bell ringing, an alarm of some sort.

'Well, I should be going,' he said. 'I'll see myself out.'

And that was that.

'I'm sorry I wasn't better company,' I said.

'You're tired, that's all. You've never liked the heat.'

We stood in the hallway, him with his hands stuffed inside his khaki pockets, and me with my arms folded tight across my chest to hold myself together, but I must've looked defensive, as though I was fed up with him.

Although he'd said he was leaving, he didn't seem like he was ready to go and in this in-between state, this awkward waiting, this not-coming-or-going, he'd usually be the one to make the first move to action, easy, confident and calm.

But he stood stock still, and looked at me, really looked at me, like he'd done in the kitchen. I didn't want to speak, and I didn't know what to say, and he didn't either, so I opened the front door and stepped outside and waited for him to follow.

I was in a bad way then, sweating and hurt, afraid Janice was gone for ever, and though I didn't want to be left alone, I didn't know how to be in this state with him watching me, and he didn't like the idea either. It was embarrassing, I think, that was the root of the problem.

'Goodbye,' I said.

'Goodbye, son. Take care of yourself.'

I'd turned to go back inside when he stepped back onto the porch and took a tight hold of me. He hugged me, long enough for me to feel what went on beneath his chest, and I closed my eyes as he held me, and it went on for a long time and there was no rush from either of us to get it over with, and I held him with the same strength as he held me.

My father let go first, but it wasn't to be rid of me. And I knew that. He wanted to say something, but didn't, and he waited, took a deep breath, took hold of my hands; his two hands over mine, like a blanket.

'I hope you can find a way out of this situation, son. I wish you luck.'

'OK,' I said. 'OK, Dad.'

Saying 'OK' said nothing. But as I held my breath, and watched him walk down the path, I hoped he realised that I wanted to say more, that I just didn't know how to take the chance.

He'd know, wouldn't he, that I was too surprised, that I was too confused to speak, that I wanted to avoid saying the kind of things that might bring my emotions to the boil, and that I was too busy shuddering to let him stay, or say anything more; that I wasn't angry with him and didn't want to see the back of him. I hope he knew that morning – that he realised – as he walked down the road – and I watched him all the way to the corner – that I loved him, because I never did get round to saying it.

REGI CLAIRE

THE TASTING

THE WOMAN SEEMED young, too well dressed for walking alone on a dusty track under the hot sun. Her skirt and blouse were watery shades of blue, boutique chic like her ethnic bag and the sandals powdered with grit. Her feet were chafed red. Her hair clung to her skin in long, pale waves. When would she finally cut it off? Stopping to wipe her face with a tissue, she took off her sunglasses, her eyes vague and uncertain in the glare. Her mobile, she had just realised, was back at the hotel.

She was lost, and she knew it. To one side of her lay a small settlement of pristine-looking apartment blocks whose lawns gave onto scrub and woodland, to the other a vastness of orchards swathed in sea-green netting, the ground beneath littered with apples and pears prematurely fallen in the brutish heat. Behind her stretched acres and acres of cherry trees. Their fruit had already been picked, with the exception of a crippled old tree, cleaved by lightning perhaps, which bore a crop of sun-shrivelled cherries pecked at by birds and sucked dry by wasps, no good for selling, but as sweet and intoxicating as wine.

Earlier, while passing through the vineyards beyond the cherry orchards, she had caught a glimpse of someone walking a dog, a long distance away. Now she thought she could hear voices from the underwater gloom of the apple trees, bouts of laughter, and she called out, though not too loudly, because the voices had sounded male. Nobody answered. Only a church bell started ringing, far away, the sound sluggish and half molten in the heat, absorbed by the trees just like they seemed to absorb the heat, their leaves when she touched them wilting and paper thin. Glancing over at the settlement, she saw no one, nothing but an empty car park, its tarmac so shiny black it shimmered near white, like the surface of a lake. She passed her tongue over her lips.

All of a sudden, up ahead on the track, two people appeared, a couple holding hands. Despite her sore feet the woman hurried towards them, then addressed them in the local language, hesitantly, aware maybe of her lack of words.

She asked the way to Village E, which she knew had to be there somewhere – she was sure she had heard the church bells. But anything seemed possible in this arid, brittle landscape, under these strange, high skies full of birds of prey that at one point had circled right above her head, their wings casting shadows that had made her shiver.

The couple were very young and probably not a couple at all. The man had one eye half closed and stared at her with the other, his lips moving clumsily to form words she couldn't understand. The girl, a big formless girl whose face looked more male than female, smiled and there were gaps in her mouth from missing teeth. Letting go of the young man's hand, she gestured to the woman to follow her as she went down some kind of access ramp towards another part of the settlement, with a big yard in the middle and buildings on three sides. A school? Behind them the man had started shouting, his tongue lolling, his bad eye squinting shut. But he stayed where he was.

When they reached the yard, they turned left, skirting the back of one of the buildings. And suddenly there were voices

– and young men seated at several tables on adjacent patios, drinking beer and playing cards. The girl with the missing teeth disappeared through a doorway. The woman waited. Tried to hide from the glances and laughter of the men, who were now staring over at her, mouthing things she couldn't make out, pointing and waving, leering with thick lips and squinty eyes. Some of them wore T-shirts, others were bare-chested, a glisten of sweat on their skin. The woman crossed her arms over her summer blouse. What was she waiting for? Who? It was like being on the other side for once, in a cage or an enclosure, a freak. When a shaven-headed man, half naked, got to his feet and started towards her, the woman's muscles tensed and she clutched her bag, ready to run. But he was pushed down into his seat.

A few more minutes passed before the formless girl reappeared. She was no longer smiling. Shrugging her shoulders, perhaps apologetically, she shook her head while behind her a tall bald man in jeans and shirt, his forearms and skull inky with tattoos, stepped out on to the patio. Everyone fell silent. When he opened his mouth, the woman expected more gaps, more thick-lipped vowel sounds. Instead his voice came smoothly, in her own language, and his teeth were perfect: white and shiny.

'Lost your way, have you?' He smiled.

'Yes,' she said, 'I want to go to the wine tasting in Village E. I'm supposed to meet some friends . . . '

The man strolled over to her, casually touched her long blonde hair with his fingertips, then nodded. 'Mhm . . . We'll be able to help you all right, don't worry.'

The woman retreated a little.

He smiled again and, addressing the young men, said something accompanied by hand signals. They all stood up as one. Like a conductor with his baton, he made them answer him in a chorus of orchestrated noise that started deep down, then slowly ascended, increasing in volume until they seemed to be ululating.

Were they singing to her? The woman felt dizzy all of a sudden, and very tired. Exhausted, really. Someone had placed a chair behind her and she sank down on it, dropping her bag. The ululating was swelling and receding in waves, soothing somehow, and she forgot she had wanted to leave as quickly as possible, to get away away away . . . Her legs had gone heavy, her arms were limp and hanging, her eyelids drooping; all she could see was her skirt rucked up high on her thighs.

She never even caught the moment when her eyes closed. There was silence all around her now as if she was quite alone, adrift once more in the vastness of the orchards, lost in the vineyards that seemed to stretch back to what had always been and always would be – some sort of eternity perhaps, an in-limbo world at best, an agony of crucified shapes at worst.

When the woman awoke, it was dark, with flickerings of subterranean light from a small opening above her and the sound of water, a stream maybe. She was lying on a hard surface, something soft and lumpy under her head: her bag. A blanket had slipped half off her and she instinctively pulled it up to her chin. She cried out, she couldn't help it.

A door opened and footsteps filled the darkness with echoes. A torch shone into her face. The man with the tattoos smiled down at her, a friendly, reasonable smile, before asking if she was all right; she'd passed out in the yard, too much sun, no doubt, so they'd brought her here to the cellar. He hoped the plank hadn't been too hard, and would she like something to eat, the wine tasting was about to begin.

'Thank you,' the woman said. 'You're very kind.' And although she was still a little dazed, she sat up, blanket around her shoulders, hands clasped around her knees. She could hear bleating outside and the tinkling of bells. There had been no sign of sheep at the pristine settlement, but Village E was a farming village, she knew and, suddenly weepy with relief, she squeezed her eyes shut.

The man's shoes rapped against the floor as he moved away. 'Take a look,' he said. 'I painted this myself – one of our previous tastings.'

The torch beam was directed at a mural of two countrymen seated at a table, drinking wine by candlelight beneath a window with a sickle moon. Behind them, leaning against a chest-high wine barrel with the lid off, were the shadowy figures of a man and a girl – the girl's head was tilted back, the man's body almost covering hers as he held a bottle to her mouth. Next to the mural hung a large photograph of the same two men seated at a table, drinking wine by candlelight beneath a window with the same sickle moon.

'Not bad,' the woman said. 'I like the artistic licence.'

'What artistic licence?' the man asked, just as a dog started barking outside, frantically.

She fiddled with a strand of hair. 'Anyway, would you mind putting the light on, please? And could I have some water?' The plank was beginning to feel uncomfortable and she groped along its edges to test the floor – cobbles, safe enough. She reached for her bag and stood up, the blanket around her shoulders.

'There'll be plenty of water later, believe me,' the man said. Then he clicked his torch on and off a few times.

The barking stopped abruptly. Light came flooding in as a wide door swung open and the big girl entered, in a dress now and much shapelier, much more feminine-looking than before, followed by a procession of the young men wearing shirts and ties like office clerks or bank managers. Gone were the slack lips and squinty eyes. Had it been the beer and sun dazzle that had caused those?

The newcomers were carrying trays with glasses and

loaves of bread; wisps of incense rose from the girl's hands. Oil lamps were brought and candles whose flames jittered spookily over the vaulted ceiling, the walls and stone pillars, over the trestle tables, chairs, pyramids of wine cases and the massive wooden barrels, some upright and serving as bistro tables, others lying on their side like beached animals. The woman went up to one and tapped it, letting her blanket fall to the floor.

'Solid oak.' The tattooed man brushed against her as he set an oil lamp on top. 'So beautifully made you could float across a lake in that. Well, almost – we haven't actually succeeded yet.' He winked at her, perhaps to show he was joking, before turning away to help the others.

Watching the shadows fling themselves against the cellar walls in an agitation of arms and legs and what seemed like horns, tails and multiple heads, the woman shivered. Why on earth had she wanted to write an article on a wine tasting? Without her mobile, she couldn't even call her editor. At least she had her camera. Might as well document her visit; some snaps for the family album, if nothing else.

She was about to zoom in on the mural when a hand blocked the lens. 'What the hell – ?'

'We don't like publicity here. House rules, I'm afraid. Underground art needs to remain just that: underground. There isn't much wine for sale anyway and we couldn't cope with an onslaught of visitors. I'm very sorry if you weren't apprised of this in advance.'

No, she certainly hadn't been *apprised* by the hotel receptionist. The woman stared back at the tattooed man as hard as she could, but her eyelids fluttered for an instant. Couldn't they make an exception? The pictures wouldn't be published, after all. She smiled persuasively and adjusted a bra string that had slipped down her shoulder.

'No exceptions,' he said. 'This is private property.' And he continued to look at her until she lowered her eyes. 'Well, now that's sorted, let's get going.' He sounded almost hearty.

Why was it always him that spoke, never any of the others? Weren't they allowed to talk? All at once the woman became aware that she could hear only guttural noises and the occasional laughter, no voices.

She strode up to the girl, who was laying out paper napkins on one of the trestle tables. 'Hello again,' she said, the foreign words coming less haltingly now. 'Thanks for getting me here, I appreciate it.'

The girl blinked and seemed confused, saying something that sounded as if she, too, had had a touch of the sun. Through the gaps in her teeth the woman could see her tongue sliding about rather like a slug. A few of the girl's words she thought she recognised, though they didn't make any sense, and she gave up, addressing instead a young man with some bottles.

'This is the wine cellar in Village E, isn't it?'

The man didn't seem to understand either and shook his head, then bent over the table to place the bottles on the napkins. Afterwards he tried to say something, his hands twitching with the effort, but he only managed a fine spray of spittle, his lips thick and slack, his eyes squinting.

The woman shrank back. A story all right, what a gift of a story she had strayed into! For a moment she pictured the headlines emblazoned across the front page of her newspaper: 'Disabled People Used As Cheap Farm Labour – investigative journalist Esme K goes undercover in a secret facility among the orchards and vineyards near Lake Geneva.'

There was a sudden commotion as everyone sat down around the tables. The woman who called herself Esme, if that was her real name, pulled her chair away from the rest for a better view of the proceedings.

'Let the Bacchanalia begin,' the tattooed man said in words

and in what must have been sign language. He smiled over at her.

'But . . . where are my friends?' she asked.

'They'll be here soon. They got lost too, it appears. It's a maze, this landscape, so many tracks traversing the vineyards and orchards that anyone might fall right off the map, even the initiated. We're still waiting for the wine grower himself . . . Never mind, they'll catch up with us eventually. They'll just have to drink faster, ha, ha.'

Everyone laughed. Everyone except Esme, who was plucking away at her skirt, which had rucked up again, exposing her thighs.

'Celina here will do the honours . . . Thanks, Celina . . . Now this one, The Alliance, is a traditional white from the region, very subtle, unique in revealing the different *terroirs*. Let's have a taste. Cheers!' And he raised his glass in celebration before taking a sip. Then he picked up one of the loaves, broke off a chunk and passed it on.

Esme glanced around. The young men were all wearing identical white shirts delicately patterned with red lines like thin trails of blood – an assembly of the national colours. As they ate and drank, they laughed and gesticulated among themselves, not paying her the slightest attention. She could tell they were deliberately ignoring her, as if they were playing some kind of game.

She gulped down her wine, ripped into her bread. It was yeasty, almost salt free, and so moist the last of the crumbs stuck to her fingers. She was licking them off when she heard the tattooed man call to her, 'Here are your friends now.'

They were being led into the cellar one at a time, blindfolded and smiling. There were five in all: a teenage boy with curls like a pirate, two men, bearded and older, and two young women, a redhead and a brunette, whose hair reached all the way down to their waist.

'These are your friends, aren't they?' he inquired.

They weren't, but Esme nodded anyway. She could play the game as well as anyone, making up the rules as she went along.

When the blindfolds were removed, the new arrivals looked about them with obvious approval, excitement even. The brunette clapped her hands and exclaimed in an exotic accent how she'd been dying to see a cellar like this. 'A *real* cellar. Like a dungeon.' She laughed, then stepped over to Esme and touched her blonde hair. 'Hey, Goldilocks,' she said, 'that's what brought you here, too, yes? You want to experience the *real* thing, not just some game on a console. You could be the princess we've come to rescue!' Laughing again, she turned to her companions, who had staring eyes with tiny pupils, like the pointed ends of knives. 'Let's play a hostage game, shall we?'

For a moment Esme could have sworn she was back in the vineyards. Trapped. They were all around her. Lines of vines marched up and down the hills, straight as columns of soldiers with their arms out, the leaves on them hissing faintly in the heat, their grapes green and heavy and sour. Lizards resembling sticks vanished without a sound, betrayed only by their quick-slinking shadows. Above her the sky had melted into a white emptiness, devoid of blue and birds of prey, and she remembered suddenly one of her first-ever assignments, an article about people working in a crematorium.

'But we're having a wine tasting,' she said, forcing a smile while trying to forget that years-ago visit to the crematorium, the velvet drapes bristly to the touch, flecked with dandruffy dust, the rubber-skin smoothness of the conveyor belt, the fingerprint smudges on the metal incinerator with its inspection opening at eye level . . . 'That's why we're all here, right? For the wine tasting?'

The brunette shrugged. 'If you insist. I'm easy.'

'Count me in,' one of the men said, and his beard seemed

to writhe like a soft little animal. 'We'll have plenty of time left afterwards. I paid for a four-hour adventure.'

Skull gleaming – had he put oil on it? – the tattooed man nodded and, indicating the empty chairs among the young men, asked everyone to sit down. His language was more formal now, more measured, almost incantatory.

Celina filled the newcomers' glasses, offered them bread. Round and round the tables she went, never stopping once. She seemed to be everywhere.

There was no chance of any conversation between the guests. They were separated by the young men, whose guttural laughs and noises were getting steadily louder, reminding Esme of their ululating earlier. Or had that merely been her imagination, overwrought and overheated like her body? Her head was beginning to spin, and she asked again for water.

'Patience,' said the man with the tattoos. 'You'll have to work up a proper thirst first.' He smiled. 'As I said, there'll be plenty of water later. I promise.'

'Where's my dog?' the teenage boy burst out suddenly. 'I want my dog!' He stumbled off towards the hulking wine barrels, perhaps to find the door. There was a crash as he fell over. He didn't get up, just started weeping drunkenly.

The tattooed man laughed. 'Don't worry about your dog. He is in good hands. No dogs allowed in here; too many legs, like yourself!'

Faster and faster the bottles kept coming: The Lovers, Harmony, Pirate's Pot, Song of the Cricket. Everyone was made to drink at least two glasses of Will-o'-the-Wisp, the house wine. When the young men's noise had crescendoed into a cacophony of echoes that chased each other round the cellar walls, bouncing off the thick pillars and multiplying, the man with the tattoos rose. At his signal there was abrupt silence.

'That's it, ladies and gentlemen, Will-o'-the-Wisp concludes the first game of the evening. Next come the hairstyles, so you can look your part and –'

'What part?' Esme grabbed her bag, hugging it tight against her chest.

'Any part you choose, really. That's the fun of this game.'

'Yes,' the redhead hiccoughed. 'Yes, yes, yes.' She seized the men on either side of her, pulling them close. 'See, Beauty and the Beasts!'

Esme's head was swimming. She felt cold suddenly, cold cold cold. She got to her feet, overturning her chair. 'I'm sorry, but I have to go.' Carefully she staggered away from all the drunken, squinting eyes, the loose, wine-red mouths swollen as if from too much kissing or biting. She expected them to stop her. But no one did.

When she reached the upright wine barrel with the lamp on top, she tripped over something. Someone. In the half light she recognised the teenage boy tangled up in the blanket, asleep on the floor – or perhaps he had passed out. At the last moment she managed to steady herself, stubbing her toes. Wild laughter. Catcalls. Then a man's arms went round her, iron strong, and a hard, stifling mouth pressed down on hers. She struggled, of course, tried to slither from his grasp. There was a tearing noise as her bag ripped, its fabric in shreds and the contents all over the floor. She thought again of the crippled cherry tree and how sweet its fruit had tasted – a forbidden kind of sweetness almost.

'Now what have you done?' whispered the voice of the tattooed man into her ear. 'Here, let me help you to a little more wine. Hair of the dog, you know.' And a bottle was slid between her lips.

Applause from the others, clapping and stomping. As Esme tried tried tried to push the bottle away, tried tried tried to push the man away, she could hear the crashing of waves, wave upon wave upon wave breaking onto a deserted coast, and she saw there were birds circling above her now, circling and diving, keen eyed, sharp beaked, powerful, scavenging for washed-up debris, gasping fish, smashed-up crab.

Later, once she had given up resisting, the crashing segued into a familiar stomp-stomp-clap, stomp-stomp-clap rhythm, and she sensed that some of the people were holding up cigarette lighters and candles.

A game, this is just a game, she told herself. It was, wasn't it? Simply a game for grown-ups. Maybe this was her initiation into the here and now, into a truly adult world. Maybe all she needed to do was allow it to happen. Enjoy it, if she dared. And why not? She pictured her article again, the letters were the size of fingers now, getting larger and larger because this story was so big, would get bigger yet as the night wore on. Still, in the most secret corner of her mind, Esme kept hoping for the wine grower, for anyone, to come and put an end to things.

But there was no end, of course. Not for her nor for any of the others in the cellar of the old mill. Idyllic, its setting had been called by some, due perhaps to the vineyards that covered the surrounding hills and the flock of sheep grazing by the nearby pond, a deep, natural pond overhung by trees.

Meanwhile the dog had been placed inside the first barrel. He was big enough for part of his head to be visible. They had muzzled him so he could no longer make any noise. But he would be exhausted anyway, after all that frantic barking earlier – barking his doggy heart out, it had sounded like. Only a faint growl could be heard now, which, as he floated further and further away, getting swallowed up by darkness, gradually subsided into a whimper, a whimper that might have been, almost, human.

DAVID ROSE

ELEANOR – THE END NOTES

I AM, AT last, only too ready to confess. It has been, over the years since her death, a bigger burden than I had hitherto realised. I am happy to relinquish it.

Hard to know how or where to begin. Perhaps obviously, with the Delius, which is also where it ended.

An unseasonal frost, thick as snow until the sun's arrest. A municipal hall with quite atrocious acoustics, agonising decay. And very hard seats. But heaven.

It's a strange work, isn't it, the Delius, one I had never cared for really? But with a wayward Nordic beauty that suited Eleanor perfectly. Right from the serenely passionate opening, she 'had' the work. Even that normally rather clumping accompanied cadenza was fleet and light.

I knew even before the concert it was hers. I arrived early, as was my practice, slipped round the side of the hall to listen through the windows to the final run-through. Always the test of an artist's mettle, as the adrenalin is just beginning to flow and the nerves are still abeyed, before sight of the audience. I couldn't see her through the high windows, curtained against the dazing light. Nonetheless, I fell in love, impossible suitor though I would have made.

And then, when she strode into the hall, pale faced, bare armed, brown hair tossed back, and stood, and I looked at her feet below the velvet skirt, I knew. You can tell so much, can't you, from a musician's stance, a violinist's especially.

Then the attack. Despite the orchestra, largely amateur, the insecure pulse from the semipro conductor, she just . . . floated through. The Scotch snap was perfection, the cadenza, as I said, and the ending, when the music dissolves into Northern light – I had to cover my ears from the crassness of the applause.

But she was there, still half caught in reverie, half radiant against that applause, face lifted, violin at her side.

I had to leave. There was Holst to follow. Mercifully not *The Planets*. I think it was the overture to *The Perfect Fool*, so, though a dedicated Holstian, I had to leave.

I didn't want to meet Eleanor that evening. I had instructed the friend who had tipped me off not to tell her I was to be present, to protect both parties from disappointment.

I decided instead to write, suggest as drily as I could the recording contract, only later to tell her what it meant to me. I was afraid, above all of gushing. God knows, I'm gauche enough without that.

I didn't, when I wrote, specify the work to be recorded, and on meeting her, we were both agreed it wouldn't be the Delius. We were both afraid the essential spontaneity would be lost in the studio. We decided instead on the Walton. But the decision at least enabled me to tell her how much the performance meant to me. I suggested we went back to it in a few years' time.

I also suggested, as a sort of emotional seal to the contract, taking her to meet May Harrison.

May had known Delius, indeed he'd written the Double Concerto for her and her sister Beatrice, and completed, with Fenby's help, the third violin sonata for May. She had by then been long retired and was being cared for by her younger sisters. There was a childlike Bohemianism about all of them – all sharing a bedroom and speaking only French to each other – that I thought would appeal to Eleanor.

So the following Sunday, after a set-to with the starter, we motored down. I sat in the garden with the sisters and the dogs (they bred them) while May and Eleanor talked and laughed and dipped into scores.

On the way home I determined that when funds permitted, in lieu of a proposal, I would commission a work for Eleanor herself.

It seemed feasible at the time. My little label wasn't doing badly. In those days, to the public at large, classical music meant Mantovani, while to the classical lovers, 'pop' music also meant Mantovani, so one could find one's niche, and recordings of light music subsidised the serious side, the 'hobby' side, as my friends liked to say.

At the time, I had just signed a pianist to rival Russ Conway, and was anticipating a modest return.

Alas, a few contretemps developed over the contract, an agent appeared out of the blue, and I barely broke even. So the commission – and the Walton – had to be filed under Action Later.

Fortunately I hadn't mentioned the commission to Eleanor, so it didn't affect our friendship. I accompanied her when I could (not musically, that is), mostly the chamber music/church hall haul, but she loved it, every recital a hurdle.

I helped too with her repertoire, made suggestions. I introduced her to the Finzi *Introit* – do you know it? A lovely work, well within the scope of amateur orchestras.

She had also taken in the Delius sonatas; they were to be

her first recording. They weren't easy to squeeze onto one LP, so I had reason to be proud as well. They attracted perceptive reviews and sold moderately well through the Delius Society.

But I was anxious, more than she, for a full-blooded concerto, a real hit. So I succumbed, brought out a record of old standbys – Parry, Elgar miniatures, Gardiner, and of course Eric Coates. OverCoates, as we called him in the trade, as his music helped more than one label to keep out the draughts. Thankfully it sold well on account of his wireless theme tunes, and at last the Walton could go ahead.

There was an instant set-back – a mix-up over the orchestral parts, the publishers sending those of the viola concerto, later justifying themselves by blaming my writing (I was, not uncommonly, between secretaries at the time), but after that it went swimmingly. Eleanor, bless her, worked so hard. She was even more of a perfectionist than I realised. She had a fierce frailty that made me worry. She was never satisfied.

Her opening was superb, the wistful *sognando* beautifully caught. But she had some difficulty with the lilting theme halfway in, due, I guessed, to nerves, poor love. I suggested we redo the passage. She wanted to replay the whole movement. I had to gently explain that although that was a luxury we could afford in the sonatas, with just a pianist to pay, orchestral time cost money.

Foolishly I told her of Klemperer's remark to his daughter when asked to put down some patching for a live recording – *Lotte, ein Schwindel.* She often thereafter used that against me, laughingly mostly. But I explained that we were *all* after perfection, engineers too. She took the point.

We did some more patching in the fiendishly hard second movement, but by the last movement she had relaxed, and I decided to allow the first take to stand.

I had thought of her doing the Walton sonata as coupling, but I decided to wind her down gently, like a racehorse, so I kept on the orchestra and we did *Portsmouth Point* and *Scapino*, Eleanor playing on the first desk.

After I had finished the master tape I asked her to listen to it with me. She refused. She said she was afraid of all the mistakes she'd pick out. She always preferred live performances where the mistakes would be carried by the inspiration of the moment, forgotten.

She asked if the patches were discernible. I answered that they weren't, that I was as much a perfectionist as she, and, dare I say it, as talented in my own field. She then said simply, 'Are you satisfied, Cecil?' I said I was. That was enough for her. She never, to the end, played her recordings.

She trusted me, do you see? And that trust made my betrayal possible.

When I think back, remember her talent, the frailty of her talent, of all talent . . .

To celebrate the release of the recording I took her to Fortnum and Mason's for tea. Eleanor, bless her, insisted on buying me a new tie, as the one I was wearing somehow got wet as I poured the tea. I still have both ties in my rack.

The record had some gratifying reviews, and sold over the months. Our only sadness was that May was now long dead; Eleanor could no longer repay her encouragement with her own success.

But she had friends aplenty, all pleased with her. We began to plan further recordings, plan her career, as they'd say today, although in those days it was just a case of getting on with the next job. And there were plenty of them now, on the strength of her acclaim.

She was widening her repertoire all the time – the Szymanowski First, his *Mythes* for violin and piano (new to me), the Fauré sonatas. And I was introducing her to some of the overlooked English works I felt it my vocation to champion.

Then came one of those serendipities that change everything.

I mentioned, apropos Delius' *The First Cuckoo in Spring*, the story of May's sister Beatrice and her nightingale.

Beatrice used to invite friends and organise weekends for deprived children at her Surrey cottage, and give outdoor cello recitals in the evenings. At one such, a nightingale responded and a duet ensued.

This happened again and again, in fact became a reliable occurrence. Word got to the BBC, who sent a van and recording engineer to tape it. It was the first outside broadcast, and later relayed round the world, at popular request.

Eleanor was utterly enchanted. She wanted to do likewise. She obtained a score of Messiaen's *Catalogue d'oiseaux*, and transcribed some of them for violin.

With some misgiving, I loaded a recorder and spare battery into the car boot, with a hamper, and we trundled down to Windsor Great Park.

A lovely hazy summer evening. She played and played but no bird sang.

Just as we were going to call it a day, a robin flew down and perched on her bow. She was childlike in her delight. Alas no song, then it flew away. But she was happy.

We had a half bottle of wine and sandwiches on the grass, in the setting sun.

We got back to the car only to find that with the weight of the recorder and the unmade road, we had had a puncture. I set to changing the wheel.

It took longer than I expected. I explained to Eleanor that being a recording engineer is not the same as repairing a car or designing the Forth Bridge. Luckily she seemed to have a knack with spanners, so, despite a little oil on her dress, it didn't spoil the trip.

On the way home I hit on the idea of getting hold of some

bird identification recordings, overlaying them with Eleanor's playing in call and response duets, and issuing them on EP.

But I felt a record needed something substantial, so I decided to have her do Vaughan Williams' *The Lark Ascending* and issue it with the bird duets on a ten-inch LP.

She was wonderful in the VW, strong and agile in the soaring notes, fragile in the climb.

In preparing the recording, I had the inspired idea of adding some snatches of actual larksong after the closing bars. I worried about complaints from the VW Society, but in the event they seemed happy. Unfortunately I did have complaints, from Messiaen's publishers over the transcriptions. The whole situation became – if I may risk a pun in a mea culpa – a messy 'un, but we eventually came to an agreement on royalties. Messiaen himself, I later heard, was charmed.

In the meantime, the record sold, sold like hot cakes, as you may remember, sold to all sorts and across the board. Apart from the money, it also made Eleanor's name, and meant she could record more substantial fare.

With the proceeds from that and an LP of a negro choir doing arrangements from *My Fair Lady* I decided to treat Eleanor to a new violin.

I had heard through contacts of one going, by William Robinson of Plumstead, an admired name in the trade. I telephoned the dealer and went down to Guildford.

Nothing has ever given me greater pleasure than presenting her with that violin. A beautiful thing, pure-toned, crackle-free varnish. It's the instrument you hear on all her recordings from then on: the Szymanowski First, the Bax, the Elgar/Walton sonatas . . .

But that is to anticipate. Before those records came that silvered cloud that changed my life. Our life.

I had promised to attend a recital she was giving in Dorking, and arrived a little dishevelled. I had contrived to lock myself out some days before, and as the landlord was away, was reduced to sleeping in my mixing studio. My cheque book being with my keys, I had sufficient readies for a pair of clean socks and a vest. My shirt I had washed in the basin and hung on a cable (it was still damp round the collar).

That was the occasion, and probably the reason, for Eleanor's proposing. What she proposed was not so much marriage as 'taking me in hand' but who was I to argue semantics?

You can imagine perhaps, though I doubt it, how I felt.

We planned the quietest of register office weddings, but somehow her friends found out and as we left the office they were waiting, armed with confetti they had made from an old orchestral score. We were showered with minims, crochets and quavers.

They told us later the score was *Bluebeard's Castle*. I said I had never been married before.

Then they dragged us to a makeshift reception in a scout hall; cold buffet with white wine and cider and impromptu performances of Mendelssohn and Bach, culminating in improvised *csardas* in which Eleanor, after several ciders, proved astonishingly uninhibited.

I know all this sounds too jolly, too joyous, for a confession, but it's important that you understand, understand what came later.

From then on we were inseparable. I was there at every concert, every curtain call, awaiting every flushed return. That year we recorded the Szymanowski, coupled with Wienawski to follow the Polish theme. Then she started learning the Bax, by way of tribute to May Harrison. But I still cherished my original ambition, and decided to fulfil it for our first anniversary.

By then Beatlemania was in full spate, but there were still

sufficient middle-aged music lovers to appeal to. I managed to secure the Joe Loss Orchestra for an album of arrangements from *Bandwagon*. I called it *Losst In Transit*, which I like to think helped it strike a chord, and it sold steadily for some months.

With weeks to spare I popped the surprise to Eleanor – a commissioned work of her own – and asked her for suggestions.

We deliberated for some time. Neither of us had any idea whom to approach. We had recently heard a concerto on the wireless by Malcom Williamson, liltingly elegiac, indeed written as an elegy to Edith Sitwell.

We duly wrote to him care of the BBC. Unfortunately he had by then embarked on an operatic follow-up to his Covent Garden success the previous year, didn't want the distraction.

Then Eleanor was told of a Polish composer living in England, living in fact on a houseboat at Twickenham, who had in his Polish past won the Szymanowski Prize. It seemed an omen.

We motored down to Richmond and walked along the towpath to Twickenham, hoping to locate him. Eleanor seemed to think if we could see a houseboat with a piano we had found him. I was dubious.

Eventually we gave up, visited Marble Hill House, and walked the twilit towpath to Twickenham Bridge.

Luckily a friend of Eleanor's who had played under him in Birmingham gave us the name of his publisher and we wrote.

His reply was charming but a little evasive. Could we specify what we had in mind? He had several works he needed to finish or revise, and didn't wish to stray far from their sound worlds.

We specified only that the violin be prominent and the forces small, a chamber work, ideally, but otherwise he had carte blanche.

What resulted was *Peripeteia* for violin, bassoon and triangle.

I must admit my heart sank when I first saw the score, but from such unpromising materials a masterpiece had been written, poignantly exploiting the contrasting timbres. In the first movement (there were only two) the contrast was between the violin's kaleidoscopically changing three-note motif and the almost static, tethered range of the bassoon's four notes; between the stridently lyrical, mercurial violin and the bassoon's phlegmatic gruffness, punctuated by the triangle's rills. I liked to liken it to Cassius Clay versus Sonny Liston, the triangle acting as timekeeper-cum-referee. But at least one of Eleanor's friends saw in it a portrait of our marriage, which rather upset her.

In the second movement (I take it you haven't heard the work), a palindromic reversal of the first also reverses the roles, the bassoon gaining a dour, conciliatory eloquence, the violin now muted, wistful, the triangle chiming metronomically throughout. And this, this – premonitory, though we did not know it – proved the more accurate portrait. But that again is to anticipate.

Eleanor, poor angel, set to and learnt her part. How hard she struggled at first, the idiom being so outside her usual range. But she mastered it. And we had found an excellent bassoonist, not the least phlegmatic himself, in fact most rehearsals ended in hi-jinks over a bottle of wine. (It was the triangle player who was somewhat dour, dry at least – a Euclidean temperament, Eleanor said.)

They premiered the work in Windsor and we recorded it the following day with, I'm glad to say, very little patching – 'quilting' as Eleanor called it.

We coupled it, for contrast, with Malcolm Arnold's *Sea Shanties for Violin and Accordion*. It didn't sell as well as we hoped, but it brought her heightened respect as an adventurous artist. I felt immensely proud, of her and of myself.

Perhaps that pride was hubris? For soon after, tragedy, as they say, struck. Actually less of a strike, more a gradual attrition.

We were trying to decide on a follow-up to the Szymanowski. Eleanor at length chose the Prokofiev First, for its similar fairy-tale quality, and I booked the orchestra and venue.

No problems showed up in the rehearsals, but the recording . . .

She was exquisite in the hushed, magical opening, agile in the pizzicato. But when the first theme returns softly on solo flute (you know the passage, I'm sure) her accompanying ornamentation was marred by a succession of sharp intakes of breath. I put it down to nerves or indigestion, or the fact that she was more closely miked than usual, and we were able, after several attempts, to patch it.

I detected it again in the scherzo, but as that is more raucous, it didn't intrude. The last movement gave me a few problems, and Eleanor seemed unusually tense, but determined to come up with a perfect take. Eventually we succeeded.

I was then taken up with the usual post-recording work, and Eleanor always made a point of practising alone, so we made no mention of it all.

But at her next concert a few months later – she was doing the Bax – I thought I heard, from the front row, the same wince. The audience hadn't seemed to notice so I shrugged it off.

A week later she gave a chamber recital of Fauré and Grieg. Then it was unmistakeable.

They say every marriage is a secret to those outside it. But to one inside it too, especially one as ill-prepared for marriage as I.

And that tragedy brings you closer. The closeness was an embrace across barbed wire. I became more solicitous, but had to work hard to hide it. Eleanor had perhaps the harder part, of pretending not to know that I knew, although in point of fact I knew very little. I tried to put it down as my overreaction to an undeserved happiness.

Eleanor carried on her fiercely independent self-hood, practising alone behind locked doors. So we kept up that embrace. Until the day I noticed the door unlocked.

I listened outside for a while to her playing, then peeped inside to catch unawares, perhaps, her hair being tossed in concentration.

The room was empty.

Full, rather, of her presence, emanating from a tape recorder. From the spool I could tell she hadn't been gone long, but could afford to be away for an hour or so. I closed the door and leant against the wall.

Driven after several drinks to the despicable, I found her diary. For that day, just a time. I traced back, those similar bald entries over several months, back to the first, of both name and time. Appointments with her doctor.

I cried in both relief and worry.

That was when the strain began in earnest. Unable to confront her with my compromised knowledge, yet not knowing exactly what that knowledge was, save from a glimpsed bottle of painkillers in her handbag, I was forced to second-guess her decisions, make tactful suggestions . . .

It was clear from her whimpers and grimaces, clear to me at least, that concerts were proving a trial, that she couldn't keep them up. How to tell her, or rather, enable her to tell me?

I put it to her that I still had so much repertoire I wanted her to 'put in the can' for me that perhaps, for my sake, she could forego live performances for a while. She finally agreed.

I knew it wouldn't be easy. Those whimpers of pain, of which I think she was quite unaware, would necessitate endless takes, tactful patching. Her views on that hardened. Needing the recording sessions as surrogate concerts, she craved whole, unblemished takes, the sweep of perfection. I had to defend the endless fiddle, the stop-and-start, the cumulative piecemeal perfection. I realised how unsatisfying that type of perfection is for an artist.

I had to argue that she was being selfish, that there is the subjective perfection of the artist, but also that of the listener, that there is the need to create, sustain, a momentary perfection to redeem the ramshackle, humdrum life of contingency that most of us live. That, ultimately, it is the achieved artifact that is important to the world, whatever the means.

We were recording the Lennox Berkeley at the time. The endless battles with the *cantus firmus* in the lento, the tears of frustration as I rejected what to her were perfect takes, wore us both down. Eventually I cobbled together a reasonable tape and we called it a day.

I insisted on her taking a break for a while, but she soon fretted to get back to work, so we started on the Prokofiev Second, to complete the set.

On the second night she went straight to bed, taking a painkiller, for a headache, she said. I went in later, watched over her bed. One hand under her cheek, the other arm thrown back, her hair floating on the pillow, she was sleeping fitfully, her lips shaping little soundless cries.

That was when I thought the unthinkable.

Next morning I stopped her a few times in the run-through of the andante, then gave her her head in the take.

At the end she looked up, waiting for the retakes. No, it's fine, I said, 'in the can'. Let's press on.

On the way home I said quietly, I've capitulated.

That evening I got out the Schwann catalogue.

It's a bit like horsebreeding, a question of pedigree. Tracing the lineage, the stables, who had studied with whom. Eleanor had studied with Warburg who had studied under Enescu who also taught Menuhin . . . And so forth.

It was, I suppose you would say today, like getting a DNA match. Not exact, but near enough to tweak.

So I obtained a recording of the work (I won't tell you whose) and, with some judicious adjustment of the balance, I spliced in the necessary passages, altered the speed a little so the graft 'took'. I would always be aware of the grafts, but I was confident that the results were no more artificial than the usual patching. It was the nearest to perfection I could achieve under the circumstances.

But what next?

Our original intention had been to record neglected works of the English repertoire – the Havergal Brian, the Britten, Holst's Double Concerto, Rubbra's sonatas. That was no longer possible. For where would I obtain the grafting stock?

I had to tactfully steer Eleanor away from that idea, persuade her of the need to prove her mettle in the standard repertoire.

Thus we did the Mendelssohn, the Brahms, two of the Mozarts. The patches, the grafts, were getting longer, but by careful choice of stock, and care in sending out the review copies, I got away with it. But for how long? Her stamina was depleting, though the resolve was still there.

Then came the moment I had been dreading. She brought up my promise to record her in the Delius. Perhaps sentimentally as well as artistically, she was determined to hold me to it.

What the hell to do? There were so few recordings to draw

on. The Pougnet/Beecham of 1946 was too well known, too distinctive. What else was there?

Then, almost in despair, I came across a reference to yours. I wrote to your company's distributor in Sweden for a copy.

It was – is – a wonderful performance. You may suspect flattery in that, but to counterfeit a phrase, plagiarism is the sincerest form of flattery.

I found it pure-toned, coolly lyrical, so similar to my memories of Eleanor's performance. And, luckily from my view, unknown outside Scandinavia.

I arranged the venue and orchestra and we began recording. I took the precaution of setting Eleanor well forward from the orchestra – the close-miking now would hardly matter.

In spirit she was inspired. But as I feared, I was able to use hardly any of it. I got her to repeat a few passages for form's sake. But the finished record was, I have to confess, almost entirely yours.

Not the opening bars, though. Those were hers, and are sublime, as I hope you'll agree. If only she'd been able to maintain . . .

None of this is meant in mitigation. I just want you to understand.

I delayed the release as long as I could, but Eleanor became increasingly impatient as she declined. I gave in, coupled it with the still unreleased Berkeley and brought it out. I sent out only limited review copies. Ironically, they were very well received, you will be pleased to hear.

It sold moderately well for a while, then went the way of most recordings – n.l.a. in the catalogues.

So it would, should, have remained, had I not been foolishly persuaded to re-release it on compact disc in her memory. That decision, and the boy's-own sleuthing in the musical press – but no! It's as well it was found out. I have opportunity to make amends, to you at least. And I'll be with Eleanor the sooner.

I hope this letter reaches you still alive.

~

Brockleby-Barr my dear sir,

How gratifying your package, I found. My eyes give trouble in these late days, so I played first the disc before reading your letter. Thankfully. For I was entranced.

Yes, they are not my opening bars, and this threw me off the scent, as you say. But how assured, how beautifully judged. And later too, the yearning, infinity pitied passages of the slow movement, so sadly lovely. The arpeggios in the cadenza, the 4/4 dance rhythms of the scherzo, so hard to make lyrical – these I admired.

Then my attention snagged (is this correct?) on the clarinet's second figure in the closing bars. He plays an A. It should have been A flat. I was reminded of a similar mistake in our recording. A coincidence? An error in the score?

And the violin's fading close – not as whispering as I would have liked.

Then I summoned my attention to your letter, to discover this was indeed my own performance. What strange elation I felt at first.

Your Scottish poet tells of the gift to see ourselves through other's eyes, or ears. This, my dear sir, is what you gave me. And how proud it made me for a time. For the praise of others is a poor substitute for one's own self-worth. And that is in normal life denied the artists. We know only the frustration, the failures, the wasted attempts.

My defence lay in giving only public concerts, in giving

up recording altogether. My recording company pressed to record my concerts live, but no. I had no wish to preserve my errors with the coughs of auditors on plastic for posterity.

I have not even played your disc again, for the same reason, in fear of all the old dissatisfactions flooding in. Within minutes of the realisation it was mine, I was remembering the difficulties of those 4/4 passages, the number of takes, the final abandonment. Also the second, and third, thoughts on the tempi of the cadenza, the linger of the close . . . All the elation rubbed away.

But for those minutes I was happy, a happiness I had not expected. I had glimpsed of freedom, a moment perfection. I was grateful.

I hope you read my clumsy hand, and that in my turn, this letter finds you still alive.

CONTRIBUTORS' BIOGRAPHIES

CHARLES BOYLE has published a number of poetry collections (for which he was shortlisted for the TS Eliot, Forward and Whitbread prizes), a short novel (McKitterick Prize, 2008) under the pen-name Jennie Walker, and two books combining text and photography (under the pen-name Jack Robinson). He runs the small press CB editions.

REGI CLAIRE is the author of the story collections *Inside~Outside* and *Fighting It*, both shortlisted for a Saltire Book of the Year Award, and two novels, *The Beauty Room* and *The Waiting*. She was born and brought up in Switzerland but now lives in Edinburgh, where she teaches creative writing at the Scottish National Gallery. She is a Royal Literary Fund Fellow at Queen Margaret University.

LAURA DEL-RIVO was born in Surrey in 1934. Her first novel, *The Furnished Room* (1961), filmed by Michael Winner as *West 11* (1963), was reissued by New London Editions in 2011. Two of her short stories have appeared online at *3:AM Magazine* and a collection, *Where is My Mask of an Honest Man*, is forthcoming from Holland Park Press. She lives in Notting Hill and runs a stall at Portobello Market.

LESLEY GLAISTER has written thirteen novels, the most

recent, *Little Egypt*, to be published by Salt in 2014. Her stories have been anthologised and broadcast on Radio 4. She has written drama for radio and stage. Lesley is a Fellow of the RSL, teaches creative writing at the University of St Andrews and lives in Edinburgh.

MJ Hyland is the author of three novels, including *Carry Me Down*, which was shortlisted for the Man Booker Prize. She is a lecturer in creative writing at the University of Manchester and co-founder of the Hyland & Byrne editing firm. Her most recent novel is *This is How*.

Jackie Kay is a poet, novelist and short story writer. Her novel *Trumpet* won the Guardian Fiction Prize and the autobiographical *Red Dust Road* won the 2011 Book of the Year at the Scottish Book Awards. She lives in Manchester and teaches at Newcastle University.

Nina Killham is the author of three novels – *How to Cook a Tart*, *Mounting Desire* and *Believe Me*. She also writes short stories and screenplays. She holds dual British-American nationality. She lived in Crouch End, north London, with her family for 15 years and has just moved to Melbourne.

Charles Lambert is the author of two novels, *Little Monsters* and *Any Human Face*, and a collection of short stories, *The Scent of Cinnamon*. He lives in Italy. Forthcoming are a psychological thriller *The View From the Tower* (Exhibit A) and *With a Zero at Its Heart* (The Friday Project), a series of 120-word texts, arranged by theme, adding up to a picture of one man's life.

Adam Lively has published four novels and also worked as a producer/director of TV documentaries. He is currently working on a collection of interlinked stories and completing a doctorate at the University of London on cognitive dimensions of narrative.

ANNELIESE MACKINTOSH's short stories have appeared in *Edinburgh Review, Gutter, Causeway/Cabhsair, Valve Journal* and elsewhere. Her fiction has been broadcast on BBC Radio 4 and BBC Radio Scotland. In 2012 she was shortlisted for the Bridport Prize and won first prize for the Unbound Press Short Story Award. She lives in Manchester.

ADAM MAREK is the author of two story collections – *Instruction Manual For Swallowing* and *The Stone Thrower* – both published by Comma Press. He won the 2011 Arts Foundation Short Story Fellowship, and was shortlisted for the inaugural Sunday Times EFG Short Story Award. His stories have appeared in many magazines and anthologies. Visit Adam online at www.adammarek.co.uk

ALISON MOORE's first novel, *The Lighthouse* (Salt), was shortlisted for the Man Booker Prize 2012 and in the New Writer of the Year category of the National Book Awards 2012. Born in Manchester in 1971, Alison Moore lives near Nottingham. Her debut collection, *The Pre-War House and Other Stories*, is published by Salt.

ALEX PRESTON is the award-winning author of *This Bleeding City* and *The Revelations* (Faber 2010, 2012). He is a journalist and critic and was a regular panellist on BBC2's *The Review Show*.

ROSS RAISIN was born in 1979 in Silsden, West Yorkshire. His first novel, *God's Own Country*, was published in 2008 and went on to be shortlisted for nine awards. His second novel,

Waterline, was published in 2011. In 2009, he was named Sunday Times Young Writer of the Year.

DAVID ROSE was born in 1949 and spent his working life in the Post Office. His debut story was published in the *Literary Review* (1989), since when he has been widely published in magazines in the UK and Canada. He was joint owner and fiction editor of *Main Street Journal*. His first novel, *Vault*, was published by Salt in 2011; a collection, *Postumous Stories*, is forthcoming.

ELLIS SHARP was born in Harrogate. His short stories have appeared in numerous fringe publications and a selection entitled *Dead Iraqis* was published by New Ventures in 2009. He is also the author of four novels: *The Dump*, *Unbelievable Things*, *Walthamstow Central* and *Intolerable Tongues*.

ROBERT SHEARMAN has published three collections – *Tiny Deaths*, *Love Songs for the Shy and Cynical* and *Everyone's Just So So Special*. An award-winning playwright, radio dramatist and *Doctor Who* screenwriter, he is currently writing 100 new stories, one each for those readers who bought the leather-bound limited edition of *Everyone's Just So So Special*. The stories are posted online at justsosospecial.com.

NIKESH SHUKLA is the author of the Costa First Novel-shortlisted *Coconut Unlimited*, an e-book about the 2011 riots, *Generation Vexed* (with Kieran Yates), and *Kabadasses* for Channel 4 Comedy Lab. His stories have appeared in the Book Slam anthology, *The Moth* and the *Sunday Times* online, and have been broadcast on BBC Radio 4. He was born in London and now lives in Bristol.

JAMES WALL has an MA in Writing from Sheffield Hallam

University and was shortlisted for the Bridport Prize in 2010. His work has previously been published in *Matter, The View From Here* and *Tears in the Fence*.

GUY WARE was born in Northampton and studied English at Oxford. He has published stories in various anthologies and his debut collection, *You Have 24 Hours to Love Us*, is published by Comma Press. He lives with his family in London.

ACKNOWLEDGEMENTS

The editor wishes to thank AJ Ashworth, Elizabeth Baines, Bernadette Jansen op de Haar and Cathi Unsworth.

'Budapest', copyright © Charles Boyle 2012, was first published in the *Warwick Review*, March 2012, and is reprinted by permission of the author.

'The Tasting', copyright © Regi Claire 2012, was first published in *Ambit* 210 and is reprinted by permission of the author.

'J Krissman in the Park', copyright © Laura Del-Rivo 2012, was first published online in *3:AM Magazine* and is reprinted by permission of the author.

'Just Watch Me', copyright © Lesley Glaister 2012, was first published in *Edinburgh Review* 135 and is reprinted by permission of the author.

'Even Pretty Eyes Commit Crimes', copyright © MJ Hyland 2012, was first published online in *Granta* and is reprinted by permission of the author.

'Mrs Vadnie Marlene Sevlon', copyright © Jackie Kay 2012, was first published in *Reality, Reality* (Picador) and is reprinted by permission of the author.

Stokes (Unthank Books), and is reprinted by permission of the author.

'The Writer', copyright © Ellis Sharp 2012, was first published in *Labyrinths* 43 and is reprinted by permission of the author.

'Bedtime Stories For Yasmin', copyright © Robert Shearman 2012, was first published in *Shadows & Tall Trees* 4 and is reprinted by permission of the author.

'Canute', copyright © Nikesh Shukla 2012, was first published in *First City*, October 2012, and is reprinted by permission of the author.

'Dancing to Nat King Cole', copyright © James Wall 2012, was first published online in *The View From Here* and is reprinted by permission of the author.

'Hostage', copyright © Guy Ware 2012, was first published in *You Have 24 Hours to Love Us* (Comma Press) and is reprinted by permission of the author.

Also from Salt

SHORT STORIES

The Best British Short Stories 2011
The Best British Short Stories 2012
The Best British Fantasy 2013
Overheard: Stories to Read Aloud

POETRY

The Best British Poetry 2011
The Best British Poetry 2012
The Best British Poetry 2013
The Salt Book of Younger Poets